SEASON OF THE FAWNS

SEASON OF THE FAWNS

by Jean Ann Williams

Love Truth Publishing

*I dedicate this book to my cousin Brian Martinho,
who is also a good friend.*

Acknowledgements

To my wonderful and smart daughter Jami, who suggested I begin the craft of writing in 1994. To my son, Jason, who is always excited for the next book. And thanks goes to my granddaughter, Morgan, for the title of this book. I'm especially grateful to my husband Jim, who has supported me emotionally in the highs and lows of writing and publishing.

Special thanks goes to Heidi von Brockdorff, Dipl.OM, L.Ac for her expertise on acupuncture. Also to Edie Sodowski for the information on traumatic brain injury. Any mistakes made in regard to TBI are mine alone.

Finally, and above all, thank You, Lord, for caring about the little and big things which happen in life on earth. You are my God and Jesus is my solid Rock.

SEASON OF THE FAWNS

by Jean Ann Williams

For everything there is a season, and a time for every
matter under heaven. Ecclesiastes 3:1

1~I SHALL NOT WANT
VALE

A RUSTY, BULLET-RIDDEN stop sign leaned at a precarious angle on the side of the road. Vale shifted her Jeep CJ7 into first gear and slowed to a halt. She checked the watch fastened on her freckled wrist. *I hope he didn't have a bad night.* After his climbing accident months ago on Watch Tower Mountain, her cousin Caleb suffered from monster headaches caused by his head injury.

She rolled into Caleb's weed-infested driveway and halted next to his pickup. The swinging bridge their grandpa Papa had built long ago stood as a guard, yet welcomed her. Her western boots hit the ground with a thud. To better enjoy the smells of the last days of autumn, she drew in a deep breath. There was nothing like dried leaves, grasses, and pine needles to permeate the air. A sudden breeze swished her russet brown hair across her high cheek bones. She giggled at the tickle.

She walked around the Jeep and opened the passenger door. From the passenger seat she grabbed a woven basket filled with Caleb's favorite foods and nudged the door shut. Vale glanced at her keys and threw them in the air. The sun glinted off them as they soared over the roll bar and plopped on the driver's seat. Perfect toss.

The basket's weight pulled at her arm, and she readjusted it. Their annual birthday hunting trip was next week. She couldn't wait to talk about the details with Caleb.

Vale's boot twisted sideways on pine cones, and she whirled her arm to gain her balance. "It's time to rake Papa's walkway." Well, now it was Caleb's. At a hurried pace, she reached the swinging wooden bridge. To steady herself, she grabbed onto the taut, rusty logging cable Papa used as a rail. At the sway of the bridge, her memories flowed. She was a little girl again at her grandparents' cottage when she used to dangle her bare feet off the bridge and stare at fish in the creek below. She always waited for a flash of silver-blue on their fins. Now as her boots crunched on pebbled ground at the other side, the past swaddled her like a thick quilt.

When Grandma Nana and Papa had passed away and gone to the Great Beyond, Caleb became owner of the cottage. Vale was more than okay about that, because their grandparents left her the hunting cabin.

She stomped up the porch steps and stood before the rough-hewed wooden door. The knob wouldn't budge. "Hey, Caleb." Her eyes adjusted to the dark interior as she peeked through the door's crisscross windowpanes. Clothes were scattered across the floor and sofa, and her gaze landed on Jimmy Bird's now-vacant cage. Even a canary can't live forever.

Her short fingernails tapped on the glass. "Hey, Cuz, I made your favorite pastrami on a French roll." She paused and raised her voice. "Extra mustard and Ma's pickled cucs."

Vale glanced at the redwood floorboards as she sat their lunch basket down. She jogged back over the bridge and fetched her key ring. She stuck the key in the door, twisted, and pushed with her hand. The old wood groaned on its hinges. The smell of must and wisdom—reminding her of grandparents—met her nose. The scent widened the ache in her chest—much like a giant hole in the earth left by the exposed roots of an old growth tree. Would her heart never heal?

She propped the piggy door stopper against the kickplate, one of dozens of pigs from Nana's collection. Vale set the lunch basket on a small entryway table and gasped. "Gross." When did Caleb become such a slob?

Her once-tidy cousin now lived in clutter, cobwebs, and leftover moldy food in to-go containers. The word slob was too harsh for someone who had been meticulous. Just one more change in his character since the fall on Watch Tower Mountain. Even worse, Caleb, the mellow guy, seemed overrun by cranky mood swings. She kicked a trail with her boots and moved clothes, a few to-go containers, and stirred more than the scent of wisdom through the cottage. She plugged her nostrils. What she really wanted was to kick Watch Tower Mountain into a pile of rubble.

The click of clawed toenails came from the kitchen, and a short, dark shape appeared in the living room. Kippy dog. Caleb's tri-Aussie whined and barked before she ran past Vale and disappeared outside. "Well, a fine howdy to you too." She chuckled. That dog always had places to go and in a hurry. But Kippy acted more wound-up than usual.

Vale moved to a closed door. "Caleb?" She pressed her ear near the door jamb. "Are you ready in there? Did you remember our picnic?" With a *tsk* of her tongue, she twisted the glass knob and shoved against the warped door into Nana's old sewing room. Closed shutters over the bay window let in slants of light that magnified the dust particles. The large sofa Caleb used as a bed filled the room, though bare of sheets and blankets. Vale furrowed her brows in a worry wart dance, stepped over his sawdust-covered jeans, and opened a door to their grandparents' bedroom.

Vale rushed to where he lay on the floor next to the bed—*Caleb*. Twisted blankets encased his body and exposed only his head and shoulders. "Caleb?" His eyes fluttered, and he murmured slurred words she did not understand. Then a moan escaped his lips. A pent-up breath whooshed from her lungs. *Get him up*. After she lugged him onto his pillow, she nudged his shoulder. "Caleb, what happened?" He shivered. She fished her cell phone from the pocket of her western-riding skirt, while her other hand laid on his light-brown hair. She punched buttons as her thumb trembled.

"911. What is your emergency?"

"My cousin needs an ambulance. 2020 Rifle Creek Road, fifteen minutes past Forest Glen Retirement Center in Forest Glen."

Twenty minutes later, the operator still had her on the phone as she instructed Vale to keep a check on Caleb's pulse and to keep talking to him. As she gave another pulse report to the operator, she broke off in mid-sentence at the sound of sirens. "They're here." Vale disconnected the call. Sobs she had swallowed down now boiled over like cowboy coffee on a campfire blaze. The medical team swooped into the room, and she leaned against the wall a few feet away. They assessed his condition. After what seemed like an eternity of questions she couldn't answer, the team carried her groggy cousin on a gurney to the ambulance.

She followed the ambulance to the hospital in Griffins Pass. Once they drove through Forest Glen and onto the freeway, she gained control of her shakes, pressed a name on her cell, and waited only seconds.

"Hello?"

"Ma!" Her voice broke, and she veered off toward the shoulder but swerved back into the correct lane.

"Is something wrong?"

"I'm okay, but it's Caleb." She nodded with her ear to the phone at her mother's next question. "Yes, he's on the way to the hospital. I found him too groggy, and he slurred his words."

Ma's words were clipped and stern. "What happened?"

Vale envisioned her ma's pursed lips and pinched brows. Tears blurred the ambulances flash of lights. She blinked. "I'm not sure. But the ambulance guy grabbed Caleb's bottle of pills he takes for his migraines from the top of Nana's dresser."

"Oh, dear Lord in Heaven." Ma spoke in a near whisper. "I hope he didn't do this on purpose."

"Ma." Vale yelled. "Don't say that just because of Papa."

"I do wish …" Ma sighed. "I'll meet you at the hospital."

"Okay." She clicked off her phone and tossed it to the passenger seat. A swell of fresh tears stung behind her nose for her papa and now Caleb.

The curving road down one of the mountain passes became a hair-pin and required her full attention. The last time she begged God for help was two months ago when Caleb fell on Watch Tower Mountain. "Dear Lord, please keep him alive." She trusted God heard. He just had to.

But she also understood His answer could be no.

VALE KEPT HER focus on a straight stretch of freeway and the ambulance's flash of lights. Caleb seemed so far away. *Could it be forever?*

It took the fourth mountain pass and into the valley to calm her jittery stomach. *Almost there.* The landscape spread before her in vivid green firs and accented were the red bark of the bold madrones. Colorful deciduous trees, their branches half-bare, dotted the landscape.

She drove for thirty miles and flicked her blinker for a right turn at Griffins Pass exit. Six traffic lights stood between her and the hospital. She memorized that when Nana and Papa had to stay at the hospital during their illnesses.

By now, Ma would be at the emergency room.

She squeezed her grip on the steering wheel at Ma's almost-comment—the thought ripped like a buck knife. *Was Papa's death really not an accident?* He'd been on various medications for different ailments, which included narcolepsy. Almost a year ago, Papa stopped his medications all at once the day before Thanksgiving. He died from a grand mal seizure.

Vale geared down to enter the ER vehicle lot. She pulled the CJ7 into a narrow space, cut the engine, and leaped from the seat. After she slipped her keys into one corduroy pocket, she patted the other to make certain her wallet had stayed in place. She strode through the automatic doors and halted. *Ma?*

There. Hunched over a water fountain. Ma's bowed legs bent, she splashed water on her flushed cheeks. *She's crying?* Very few times had she seen Rodell Cutter gush—happy or sad. Vale learned there were body languages to gauge Ma's emotions. This time, Ma was beyond upset.

Ma wiped her hands on the back pockets of her jeans and swiveled. The two women met in the middle of the room where Vale launched into her ma's arms. She sniffed. "How soon until we hear?"

"I checked in with the receptionist." Ma brushed at her wet cheeks. "They have to stabilize him."

Vale blinked. "Stabilize?"

"Yes. Caleb could be in bad shape if he took more than he should have of his medication."

She clenched her fingers and a squeal rose from the back of her throat. Would Ma never quit?

"Don't cause a scene, Vale. You know as well as I do that at the first sign of a migraine, Caleb's medication is meant to stop it. Make it go away. If he takes too many, though, who knows?"

She raked her stubby fingernails through her hair.

Ma grabbed her hand and pulled her toward the French Brothers coffee hut. "I'll get us hot drinks."

She relaxed her palm within Ma's and moisture blurred her vision. It seemed Ma was in a moment of compassion. She knew Ma loved Caleb. It was not that. But when Papa died, her mom had erected an even higher wall around herself.

They found a quiet table, their drinks in hand. Vale concentrated as she sipped her mocha. She had to talk about what happened. From before. "Caleb hasn't done well since he fell on Watch Tower Mountain."

"No, he hasn't. And his migraines and mood swings disturb me."

"Then you noticed his change, also."

"I have."

"I pray our yearly birthday hunting trip will change things for him." Vale swallowed another mouthful of the rich liquid. "You know, perk him up."

"You should cancel."

Vale leaned forward with a jerk. Mocha sloshed over the rim of her paper cup. "It's not for a whole week." She wiped at the moisture on her skirt. "I'll nurse Caleb back to health before then."

"It wouldn't be safe for him to ride his horse, carry his pistol, and even walk the steep trails."

She pursed her lips. "But."

Ma sighed, long and slow. "Don't start."

"He can't miss our yearly hunt. It would be like a surrender to his troubles, and Caleb's not a quitter." A knot formed in Vale's throat, and she swallowed another gulp of her drink. "I haven't told you, but he's skipped several worship services since his accident. And I think it's because of his pain." She drew in a deep breath. "That's *why* I know he needs some kind of normalcy, Ma. This trip will be good for him. Give him time to relax."

"I hope you're right. I miss his usual good nature." She squeezed Vale's arm. "I've learned we can push people to their limits."

There it is again. She means Papa. "You'd be grumpy too if you fell and hit your head on a rock."

"Mrs. Cutter?" The receptionist called from behind her counter.

Vale shot from her chair.

Ma hurried around the table, circled an arm around Vale's shoulders, and they walked toward the lady.

The receptionist smiled. "I'll show you to Mr. Cutter." She pointed. "Meet me at the double doors to your right."

Vale reached for Ma's hand, and they both hung on.

A NURSE STOOD outside the closed curtain.

Vale touched her chest. "I'm Caleb's cousin, Vale, and this is my mother, Rodell."

"I'm Sandy." The nurse looked from one to the other. "You're the next of kin?"

Ma nodded. "My husband and I adopted him when he was ten years old.

The nurse raised her brows. "Caleb had a close call with his medication."

"Was it intentional?"

Intentional? Vale glared at her ma.

"The small amount we pumped from his stomach?" Sandy let go of a long breath. "It's hard to tell, except his dose directions say to take only one."

"Caleb would never harm himself." Vale winced and hoped.

Sandy rested the clipboard of Caleb's information against her chest. "Regardless of why he took too many, he did overdose."

A sensation of ice water raced along Vale's spine. She locked eyes with Ma. "May I go in first?"

Sandy touched Vale's arm. "He's exhausted and sore because his stomach's been pumped. He probably won't feel like talking."

She moved closer to the curtain. "Okay."

Ma clasped her hands together and angled her chin. "Don't tire him with a hundred and one questions."

She separated the drape with a swish along the metal rod, breathed in, breathed out, and forced a pleasant expression. For Caleb.

2~GREEN PASTURES
CALEB

A RUSTLE OF fabric startled him, the noise all too similar to the flap of wings.

The mountain came to mind. The pain. The buzzards. Even though he stuffed the memory deep into the folds of his brain, he shuddered.

As he opened his lids, Vale had slipped through the divide of curtain. Her way-too-round eyes said he'd blown it now. *She's scared.* She stood over him, and one of her tears drip-dropped on his arm. Her calloused fingers touched his cheek.

He attempted to settle higher on the stiff pillow. His gut wrenched in pain.

"Don't move."

He furrowed his brows as he lowered his lashes. "Yes, sir, Miss Bossy Pants."

Chair legs raked across the tiled floor and drew closer. "Stop it, you lug head."

Was there a smile to her voice? The idea to grin at Vale came to him, but he couldn't muster it well enough to make it real.

"I was the one who found you." Her voice softened. "I have to know, Caleb." His eyelids pinged open. "On purpose or accident?" Her green eyes widened.

He pulled his stare away to focus on the cream-colored walls. "Does it matter?"

"No. Yes." Vale sniffled. "You'll always be my favorite cousin."

He couldn't even manage a snort. "I'm your only."

Why did life have to dump him on his head?

Literally.

Her sniffles grew more intense.

"Don't get sappy."

"Don't you tell me how to feel, Caleb Josiah." Vale peered into his eyes. "We'll get through this one way or another," she whispered.

He opened his mouth ready to fire back but winced instead. "Man. It feels like they did more than pump my stomach." Even to swallow seared like a forest fire.

"Now, listen." She stretched her shoulders as was her habit when she wanted to make a point. "I've already told Ma. I'll stay at your place with you for at least one night."

He gave her the stink eye. At least he could squint. She raised her hand, her index finger trained at his nose. "No. Arguments."

"You're not my mother." Caleb's muscles were as exhausted as though he had stacked a winter's supply of wood. Without a break.

"Someone needs to help you get well."

There's no help. He zeroed in on a black speck on the ceiling. *No one understands.* The pain in his head? Once in a while it became bearable, like the stings of the first warmth indoors from too long in the snow. "Don't do this for me." Moisture burned behind the bridge of his nose. He would not cry. But a bubbly sob rose from his chest.

"Mister Caleb." She tapped his shoulder. "It's like you're in a prickly patch of berries. Remember how it was as kids? You always saved me from the thorns?"

He blinked.

Hurried footsteps slowed outside the closed curtain. A man walked, a stethoscope draped around his neck. "Mr. Cutter." He nodded. "I'm Dr. Peterson." He reached out and shook Caleb's hand. A soft palm against his calluses. The doctor glanced from him to Vale and back again. "Is this Mrs. Cutter?"

"No." He curled his lip into a snarl. "More like my *mother*."

The doctor's mouth twitched.

Vale moved to make room at Caleb's bedside. "We're cousins."

Dr. Peterson's gaze remained on her, and the skin around his brown eyes crinkled. "Well, I need to talk with the patient." He pointed at her. "Does your *mother* stay or go, Mr. Cutter?"

He averted his eyes to avoid her reaction. "Go."

"Alrighty, then. I'm gone."

Dr. Peterson stared at her as she disappeared behind the curtain. He cleared his throat and patted the side of Caleb's bed. "What happened with you and the migraine medication?"

"I know what it looks like." His shoulders stiffened. "I guess I was too foggy brained to know how many I was taking."

"Okay." The doctor sat in the chair beside the narrow bed. "I'm all ears."

"I'm sick of the pain. It becomes so bad that at times I can hardly string two words together."

"How long have you been taking the medication, and what led to you needing it?"

Caleb explained about his fall on the mountain two months before. How he hit his head on a large rock. He left off the part about how scared he was when buzzards flew too low over him. That fear caused him to claw his way back to the top of the mountain. His pain so great, he rested only to vomit. "I haven't slept worth spit since then." He drew in a deep breath. "Last night, I awoke to intense pain. I remember that I went to my dresser and popped the cap on the bottle. That's about it."

Dr. Peterson nodded. "Listen, Caleb, I suggest you set out one pill next to your bed and put the rest in a medicine cabinet."

"A hard lesson learned." This was what his papa said often in Caleb's growing-up years.

He stood. "Have you had any other symptoms, like your facial muscles have drooped?" He drew closer and studied Caleb's face. "You look okay there. How about your memory? Is it as good as before?"

Caleb thought a moment. "I have been a bit forgetful, but I thought it was from the stress of pain."

"Well, yes, but a traumatic brain injury can also affect the memory. Do you have mood swings, anxiety/ and or depression?"

His nerves jumped at the doctor's bold questions. "Sometimes but, again, I thought I was wrung out from the pain."

Dr. Peterson wrote on Caleb's chart. "Has your neurologist recommended physical therapy?"

"Yes, but I've been in my busy season at work. I'll begin that soon."

Dr. Peterson studied Caleb's chart and wrote some more. "What is it you do?"

"I'm a woodcutter."

He glanced up. "I see. You need to stop such a strenuous occupation."

"I can still work like before. No problem."

"You can but should you?

Caleb puckered his mouth. No way would he quit woodcutting.

The doctor leaned closer. "Off the record, of course, but my neighbor is an acupuncturist. He has shared a few stories of how his techniques help folks."

"Can it help me, you think?"

He craned his neck toward the shut curtain, and then stared at Caleb. "I've gone to him for some of my own ailments. It had worked, so I believe it's worth a try for you." He winked and put out his hand.

Caleb reached across his chest and gripped the doctor's palm.

"God bless you." Dr. Peterson's tone grew soft. "And mind your mother, ah, I mean cousin." His eyes gleamed. "I do hope to somehow, someday, see her again, other than here."

"You sure about that, sir?" He chuckled. "She can be a bit much, and she's only nineteen, until next week."

The doctor rose from the chair. "And I'm only twenty-eight, so not so old." When he reached the curtain, Dr. Peterson pivoted and faced him. "If this happens again, by law I have to file a suicide attempt." He raised a finger. "Make an appointment to see your primary doctor. He'll get a notice from the hospital's portal with details of my report."

Caleb jerked when a stab of pain shot along his temple. "Yes, sir."

The doctor stuck his head back in from behind the curtain folds. "On a lighter note, what is your *mother's* name?"

"Sunny Vale. We just call her Vale." He smirked. "You might want to reconsider your thoughts. Firecrackers can come in short packages and burn ya with their words."

PAIN GROUND THROUGH his gut. Where was that nurse? He had to leave.

He sighed when Vale and Aunt Rodell came in. Rodell placed his hand between hers. "Son—" A sob wrinkled her features.

He gripped her fingers. "I'm sorry I worried you both."

Vale leaned over him. "If there was no big secret like you did it on purpose, then why did I have to leave the room?"

He let go of Aunty's hand. "'Cause you know how to smother a guy."

"Well," she waved a hand as though to swat a fly, "I hope the doctor was helpful."

"Yeah, and blunt."

She raised a brow and leaned closer. "As the doctor passed me, he winked."

"At you?"

A blush brightened her cheeks, and he knew her answer. She wrinkled her nose right when Nurse Sandy popped in with a whack at the curtain. "You're free to go, Mr. Cutter." She held the clipboard for him. "Just sign your name."

He scrawled above the line, Caleb Josiah Cutter. Vale grabbed his clothes and piled them on his chest. "Let's get out of here."

"He needs privacy." Aunty poked Vale's arm.

Once they left, Nurse Sandy assisted him into a sitting position and loosened the string in the back of his gown. His gut cramped, and he gulped down a wave of nausea. *Oh, Lord, I'm whooped.* He shaded his eyes with a palm. As the nurse chatted, Caleb worked hard to not puke.

"Are you nauseated?" Nurse Sandy's voice grew too loud, which caused another sharp pain through his head.

He gulped back saliva and hunched his back. He took deep breaths and prayed *help*. The room whirled.

"Breathe deeply, Caleb."

When the nausea passed, he finished dressing, though heat radiated from his face at the effort. The nurse opened the curtain, and there stood Vale and Aunty a few steps across the hall. They hurried to him. Each woman grabbed an arm, and he relaxed. For right now, he needed their help.

3~LEADS ME
VALE

"BYE, MA." AT the hospital curb, Vale kissed her cheek. "I'll call you when I get Caleb settled at the cottage." She glanced at him where he sat in the Jeep.

Their seatbelts buckled, they now headed through town and north on Interstate 5. She stole glances to see if she could gauge his pain—tension left her shoulders with a sigh—his arms stayed relaxed at his sides. *Thanks, Lord.*

She opened her mouth to ask a question. But just as fast clamped it shut. She would not smother him … at least she'd give it her best effort.

A light rain spattered the windshield. *Glad I pulled over the canvas top.*

He stretched in his seat. "I'm starved."

His voice startled her. "I'll bet." As the sun peered through the clouds, she reached for her sunglasses. "Let's stop in Cougar Creek and get deli. They've got the whole wheat rolls I like." She tapped the wheel. "That is if you feel like a sandwich."

"Nah, I better eat oatmeal at home. Did you make sure Kippy was locked in the house before you left?"

"Well. No." She tightened her grip on the wheel. "She ran past me and out the door when I got inside."

"She'll show up." He yawned. "Kippy's an explorer."

She inhaled. "Caleb?"

"Yeah?"

Did she dare discuss this? "I got to thinking. About your life and all you've been through."

Caleb crossed his arms. "My life?"

She tilted her head. "What you lost and all."

"I miss my folks if that's what you mean."

She glanced at him. "What about your migraines?"

"That is my current problem."

In an elevated climb, she stepped on the pedal and passed a semi at a crawl along the shoulder of the freeway. "Should we forget about our birthday buck hunting trip?" She cringed as the words left her mouth. Oh, how she wanted, how—how they both needed—to keep with their plans. A week-long get away and to bag a buck or two.

"Dunno. Let's see what happens."

She eased off the accelerator and geared down before a downhill curve as she passed the Sunny Vale exit. Her namesake, also her birthplace, were both a part of the history of the Oregon Trail. She was born on a kitchen table in a miner's creek-side cabin. Her ma told her the table was padded and made it easier for her dad to catch baby Vale. As she landed in his hands, she expelled a loud squall and her fists swung like a boxer.

Her parents said she was a sunburst on a snowy night.

Caleb yawned again. "Right now I want soft, warm food. Sleep too."

"Okay." She flipped a strand of hair behind her ear. "If we do take our trip, do you want to stick close to the cabin? Or bring the horses?"

"We better take the horses." He coughed, pulled a hanky from his sturdy coat pocket, and blew his nose. "I haven't ridden Storming in a while. Not since I fell on the mountain."

She let out a breath, though she did not realize she had held it. "I've been riding him, so no worries. I'll get us packed with supplies just in case we can make our trip. I'll take care of tack and the horses." She signaled for a right turn off Interstate 5 and onto exit 80. "You just rest, Cuz."

He wiggled in his seat as though he needed a more comfortable spot. "I'll help."

"No, no, I can handle it." She focused on the sharp turn in the road. "Besides, don't you have to finish your wood order? If you're able, that is."

"I'm not an invalid." He crossed his arms over his chest. "I can do it."

"I know. I know." Her fingers tapped a rhythm on the wheel as she exited the freeway. At the four-way flashing red light, she stopped, turned left toward the town of Forest Glen, and accelerated. Her muscle's twitched. So he still *wanted* to go on the hunting trip next week. *Now we'll see if he can.*

She downshifted to a crawl as they approached the lumber mill. On her left, rows and rows of stacked logs covered a half block. These waited for the machines to peel off the bark to turn into usable lumber. The Jeep continued on by the yard where they loaded finished lumber onto train flatbeds.

Forest Glen was full of history. Papa, born and raised there, worked in the lumber industry until he retired. As he told it, seventy-five years ago, eleven small to medium-sized lumber mills produced wood products which helped the growth of Southern Oregon. Now only two large operations owned by one family kept the community alive.

She slapped the blinker handle, made a right turn on Rifle Creek Road, and approached the plywood mill. The smoke from the stacks belched poisons—

something which Papa lamented. Her knuckles gripped the wheel. *This topic died with Papa.*

Caleb made a movement. He planted his palms on the sides of his head. She understood his silent language. *Lord, please give him rest today. In Jesus' name, I ask.*

She gave him a quick sideways glance as he changed position and gazed at the ranches and farms. Vale knew without looking there were names on mailboxes of the folks who settled onto large sections of land around the late 1800s. The property, and even some of the old houses that still stood, were inherited generations ago. She passed an impressive sheep ranch and read the Hissong name on the mailbox for the millionth time. *His song like God's song?* They were German folks, and sixty-nine-year-old Mrs. Hissong still worked the ranch alongside her sons, Rory and Cory, and even helped shear the sheep.

Vale stopped at a narrow dirt road and put the Jeep into four-wheel drive. Not because the Jeep couldn't take the climb necessarily, but because she enjoyed the near-growl of the engine and the feel of tires as they gripped the road. Soon enough, she swerved into the graveled drive and stopped at the swinging bridge.

Caleb yawned. "Home sweet cottage."

"Yeah." Vale got out of the vehicle and stretched. Bull Creek waters had risen, thanks to a recent rain storm. She pointed. "Look. Egrets."

"Sure enough." Caleb came round to her side of the vehicle as two white egrets glided over the water with their five-feet wing spans.

She shut her driver's door, and he nudged her elbow and pointed his chin at the Jeep. "Go home."

"No. I won't." She blinked, "I'm here to stay, Caleb." She walked past him.

"I'm a big boy, you know."

"Yeah?" She whirled round. "In pain and no one to take care of you. So it's settled."

"Vale." He raised his voice as she hurried to the bridge's gate.

She halted her steps, crossed her arms, and faced him. "Oh, for heaven's sake."

"Don't miss work. Get us ready for our trip to Papa's cabin." He spread his hands in front of him. "I already feel limited since the fall, and I need to prove I can be alone and okay."

His figure blurred before her. Two dots of moisture released and trickled.

He approached her and squeezed her shoulder. "Silly girl. Really, I'll be all right." His dimpled smile softened her as always. How many times had he talked her down from a temper tantrum? Or a climb up a tree he thought was not safe? How about the moment they received word their papa had died? The corners of his mouth turned down, he had said, "He's gone to the Great Beyond, Valie."

She bowed her head and cried until she hiccupped. His other hand cupped the opposite shoulder, and he hugged her. She willed herself to stop, and her breath shuddered. "Caleb, please." She spoke into his plaid shirt. "Don't worry me."

"I'll call my doctor when I get inside." His arms fell to his sides. "They're good about a quick appointment since my tumble on the mountain." He cocked his head. "I feel a little better now."

"If you're sure." Vale untied the bandana from around her neck and wiped her nose. "I'll get us ready back at my place."

"Good." He tapped her chin. "It'll be a fun trip at the cabin. Just like always."

A wave of emotion coursed through her again, and she rolled her misty eyes up to the clouded sky. "I'm *such* a baby."

"Me too, then." He swiped at his lashes. "It's been a hard day."

"Will you miss Papa not taking us?"

His Adam's apple bobbled. "You know it." His voice cracked.

She gripped him in a fierce hug. "Sometimes— sometimes I wish we were kids again. And . . . and Nana and Papa were still here."

There was his dimpled smile again. "We're not children anymore."

She fisted her hands in her skirt pockets. "I can keep Papa and Nana close to my heart."

"As will I, Sunny Vale."

He opened the gate and crossed the bridge on what seemed steady legs. She hoisted herself into her rig and clicked on the key. "God, please take my place here. You'll do a better job, anyhow."

Her body relaxed when she gave her request to the One who knew all and could do all.

4~STILL WATERS
CALEB

THE CHAINSAW SPUTTERED and died as it clicked. "Doggone it." His papa's Stihl saw had never before given him trouble. He looked down at his tail-waggin' dog. "Kippy, this thing's forty or so years old, girl, so maybe the saw misses its old owner." She thumped her tail faster.

Caleb reached across the seat of his 4x4 long-bed pickup and grabbed a smaller backup saw. He pulled back the rope, and it came to life in a tinny *chug a chug*. His thumb worked the button and the saw revved. It wasn't Papa's large Stihl, but it would get the job done, even if a bit slower. And maybe Dr. Peterson wouldn't object as much. Caleb laid the chain of teeth into the V cut he had started. His saw finished the cut at the base of the red barked madrone tree.

Pop!

Crack!

He switched off the saw, cupped his hand around his mouth and hollered, "Headache!" He hauled himself out of there as Papa had taught him. Another *crack!* It echoed like a lightning strike. The tree split from its trunk, screeched, and shook the ground when it landed.

From behind his pickup, he noticed the tree fell in line with the angle of his expert cut. And also, like Papa always did, he slapped his palms together and spit on the ground. "Bingo."

The madrone lay like an elegant giant between two fir trees. He raised his hands to heaven. "Thanks, Lord. Another beauty for next year's customers." A pain stabbed at his temple. *No, no, no.*

Kippy's barks carried beyond the tree line, and Caleb pressed fingers to his head. "Cornered a skunk, did ya?" The pang warned him of a wallop of a migraine, and he retrieved his pills from the glove box. He took one and kept still and waited. When minutes passed minus the pain, he figured he better get back to work.

The rope of Papa's saw became taut as he pulled, and the Stihl roared to life. The old wood ripper just needed a rest. He whacked off limbs, exchanged the heavy-duty saw for the lighter one, and cut the smaller branches. After the de-limb process, the tree would stay on the ground until later when he'd cut it into smaller rounds. But not too long of a wait. He studied the teeth on his chain. Still sharp.

He walked the few yards to the madrone he cut in rounds months ago. Yep. Seasoned and ready to split for the last of what old man Mr. McCullough needed for a full winter supply of firewood. Caleb readjusted his cap. Some pieces were shortened in length for the old man's smaller stove.

Caleb twitched his nose. Putrid. Rotted fish. He eyed the wooded area, because this meant one thing. His bear tag and hunting license were safely tucked in his wallet, and he reached into the back seat of his pickup for his Hoyt bow.

Maybe today he would bag a bear to replenish his supply of bear jerky and sausage.

Caleb buckled on the arrow release to his wrist and snagged the hook end to the bowstring. Slow as a sloth, he moved toward Kippy and her frantic bark. The stench grew stronger. *Where's the bear?* He scoured an area near where his dog kept at her fit and continued to walk toward an old, raised stump. On one knee he knelt beside it, his other boot flat on the ground, knee bent. He rested one end of the bow on his thigh without drawing, but at the ready to raise higher and aim.

Branches broke. Leaves crunched. The bear snuffled and huffed as though he smelled the ground. *Mushroom hunting?*

Then.

Quiet.

The bruin grunted.

"Yes," Caleb hissed. As the animal shuffled again, cinnamon-colored fur appeared between the spaces of trees. He raised the bow, where it now rested in his left hand in a loose cradle between thumb and index finger. To follow the bear's movements, he took aim. *Wait for it.* He would not pull back the string. Not yet. He waited to make certain of a perfect shot, and that the bear was not a yearling. The bear growled. At that, he had his answer. Experience taught him an aggressive growl meant full-grown maturity. But wait. Was it a mama and her cubs? If there were cubs, wouldn't they have made themselves known by their hoarse whining? At last, the bear appeared from behind some Manzanita shrubs and moved into full view. The bruin halted, sniffed the air, and turned its head to stare at Caleb, his beady, brown eyes too small in his face.

Air exploded from the bear's mouth, and the sides of his jowls flapped. His long, sharp teeth *clacked, clacked, clacked.*

Hold still, big guy.

He pulled back on the string. The bear stayed in the bow's line of sight, for a broadside, vital organs, double lung shot. Shoot to kill. A wounded bear became a killer.

Kippy jumped from around the bushes, a few feet from the bruin. Without a doubt, if there had been a cub or two, the dog would have flushed them out by now. She barked and snarled like a mad dog as Caleb released his arrow for the best shot. Kippy's intrusion caused the bear to jerk back. The broadhead arrow soared between its neck and front leg. The bear disappeared into the trees.

In frustration, he exhaled. "Kippy." He stood and whistled two tweets between his finger and thumb. "C'mere, girl."

Kippy scampered over a fallen, rotten tree and yipped. She circled around him, sat at his feet, and lolled out her tongue. He pointed. "You blew my shot, young lady." Her stump of a tail swished. He bent and patted her head. "You're forgiven. At least it was a clean miss and not a wounding shot."

Caleb loaded the saws, gas can, and oiler. Tomorrow after his doctor's appointment, he'd finish splitting the madrone logs on the splitter. He *had* to fill this order before his hunting trip. After he almost took down the bear, the experience set off a spark. Now he really wanted to go on the hunt.

Before he jumped into his pickup, he glanced at where the cinnamon bear had stood. He shook his head. *I could taste the jerky.*

AS DOCTOR ROGER read the hospital report in silence, his lips moved. "Okay." He stared at Caleb. "You have tried two medications since your fall accident two months ago."

"I can't get a good night's sleep either, so it's not helping."

"Your occupation is wood cutter?"

This is what he should be doing instead of discussing medications. "Correct."

The doctor murmured. "Hard labor." He took off his glasses and nibbled on the tip of the earpiece. "It could be dangerous to handle sharp tools when you're not sleeping well."

Caleb clenched his jaw. "I won't change occupations, sir. Since I was age ten, I've worked with my grandfather in the woods. He trained me, and I have his equipment and customers. Twenty in all. I want you to help me cope until I get better."

"Okay, then, you need something stronger for the pain."

Caleb leaned toward the doctor. "What?"

"It's used to treat depression."

"Wait, wait." He crossed his arms over his chest. "I'm not depressed. Ask anyone. I'm the happiest guy around." He lowered his gaze. "Or I was until my injury. And even if I'm not happy, I don't need this kind of cheer."

"Let me explain. This newer drug has proved positive results in trial groups. It has shown to alleviate migraines at best and numb the pain to bearable at worst."

Caleb squirmed. "What are the side effects?" He had to get back to the woods.

The doctor raised his chin. "

Most of them rarely happen." He looked at this watch. "I've got another patient. I can write the prescription, and if you decide against it, don't fill it. But if you choose not to use this prescription, come see me again so we can figure out what else may be best for you."

"What about physical therapy?"

Dr. Roger handed him the prescription slip. "That's an option, of course, and I think a good one. But it means time off of work."

"I can't right now, but I could once my hunting trip is over." He slipped off the table and his boots thudded on the floor. He shook the doctor's hand. "Thanks, Dr. Roger."

A short wait later at the vacant receptionist's desk, a young woman appeared. Someone he'd never met before. When she stopped in front of Caleb, her head leaned to the right. Brows arched over her wide-eyed expression.

Was she a flirt?

She grinned and exposed pink braces wrapped along her upper front teeth. "Hi."

Yep. Caleb's heart skip-a-dipped. "Hello."

She glanced over his paperwork. "I'll print the medication's fact sheet, Mr. Cutter."

Or maybe not a flirt moment, but what was it that passed between them? A zing? A zap? Or his imagination?

She entered the information, and the printer spat out papers. Caleb gave her a fifty-dollar bill. "Can you bill me for the rest?"

"Yes." The printer stopped. She lifted the papers from the tray and handed him the medication information.

As she worked at her computer, he zeroed in on her ginger hair. Shiny, loose curls fluffed across her shoulders and spiraled. His fingers twitched. He imagined his hand coiled through all that hair.

Were the waves as soft as corn silk? He blinked. Did she just speak?

The corners of her eyes crinkled. She handed him a printed receipt.

He cleared his throat. "Are you new?"

She tipped her chin in a half nod. "Yes, sir."

Through the opened window between them, he extended a hand. "I'm Caleb."

"I know." She pumped his, and her palm felt smooth. "That's what it says on your chart."

Heat crawled along his neck. *Duh.* He let go of her hand.

"I'm Cherry. They've ordered a name tag for me but it's not in yet." She looked behind him.

"Is that a nickname?"

"No." She touched a lock of her ginger hair. Someone behind him cleared their throat. She leaned forward and whispered, "There's a line behind you, Caleb."

"Sorry." He waved. "See ya, Cherry."

Splashes of a blush rose to her cheeks. "Do you need another appointment?" Her eyes grew wide, again.

"No." But her flushed face gave him courage to one day see her outside of her work. How could he maneuver such a wonderful thing? He walked around a group of people and in between the chairs where patients flipped through magazines. Determined to figure it out, he twisted to catch another peek. The next patient blocked part of her face, but from what he could see, the flush remained on her pretty features. On his way out, he jumped and slapped the top of the door frame. This jarred his head, though, for once, he didn't care too awful much.

He walked out the door, halted, and poked his head back inside to peer at the pretty receptionist. Her head tilted. Was she staring at him? Caleb winked.

Cherry's lashes fluttered to the gallop of his heartbeat.

HE SAT IN the cab of his pickup and read information about the medication. Not only was it another relief medication—so he had to take it at the onset of a headache—but the side effects. *Whoa.* Nausea, depression, blurred vision, just to name a few. "Big decision."

After he read the scary stuff, his shaky hand took a couple of tries to fit the key into the ignition. Would it hurt to try it? He wanted his life back. The word trial came to mind. He relaxed. If it didn't work, he'd quit. Yep. That would work. Caleb sighed in relief.

When his pickup engine hummed to life, he thought of a more pleasant topic. Pretty Cherry.

How could he feel so sure about her at one meeting? He shook his head and went over their conversation as he drove from the doctor office's parking lot.

At the other end of town, he slowed and pulled into the pharmacy entrance. He realized Cherry reminded him of the Red Hots candy he enjoyed as a kid. It was what she said when he'd told her his name. *That's what it says on your chart.* And her eyes had gleamed in mischief.

Now his fingers tightened around the prescription in a too-long line. Finally, in the cash register line he exchanged hard-earned money for the medication. The pharmacist lady discussed the drug with him and handed him the printout of all the side effects. She lowered her glasses on her nose and stared at him over the frames. "No matter what—" And she proceeded to tell him news he hadn't expected. He almost covered his ears.

Caleb walked on wobbly legs back to his pickup. He wouldn't blame Cherry for not telling him. That was the doctor's job. His freedom of choices snagged. Should he take a chance? What if he had a reaction? What if he was one of the statistics where it does more harm than good? Caleb fisted the printout into a ball and tossed it in the back seat.

On the drive home, many of his thoughts pounded out the side effects. His throat had as many kinks as Bull Creek below his cottage. He scratched the top of his scalp as his mind flip-flopped. Why not wait one more day to figure out whether to try the medication as a trial? His knuckles relaxed on the steering wheel. *Yeah, no rush.*

Caleb's gut rumbled. In Forest Glen, he stopped at Finger-Lickin' Cafe and ordered a to-go chocolate shake, bacon cheeseburger, and a large fry. The bag of warmth and fried smells now sat on the passenger seat. To prepare his sensitive stomach for the greasy delights, he drank half of the shake first. Vale did not approve of his fast foods. He twitched his mouth. She was a bossy one, but he knew she did it because she cared.

By the time he arrived at his cottage, the fries, burger, and the ice-cream had settled in his gut. He unlocked his storage shed and rushed to load his wood-cutting equipment into his pickup. Papa's log splitter on wheels was easy to maneuver through the open double doors. He backed the pickup to the splitter and attached the coupling to the ball. Kippy barked twice. "We're outta here, girl." That dog sure could dance and yip until he opened the driver's door. She leaped into the front seat.

Once inside the cab, he ticked off his mental list of needed tools. He stopped when he got to his extra chain saw. He double-checked the back seat. It sat right there between an extra pair of gloves and the crumbled list of side effects. His heart sped and he closed his eyes. He had already decided to pray about the medication, even as a trial. But determination to feel normal again won.

He would go for his self-made trial.

5~RESTORE MY SOUL
VALE

BOXES OF SUPPLIES and pantry foods were scattered across the medium-sized bedroom. A few more days and Caleb and she would leave for Papa's hunting cabin in the coastal mountain range of their state of Oregon. She pulled on her boots, tucked in the cuffs of her jeans, and peered in the bathroom mirror. "Ah, phooey." She blew air through her mouth, and her lips fluttered. "Not another zit." A dab of foundation on the ugly spot would cover it, but she wondered if she'd ever move from the pimple stage.

Her ma kept telling her it was something she was eating. Weren't mothers always right? *Not about Papa.*

"Gotta go." Ma peered into the opened doorway. "Have a good day."

"You, too, Ma." She moved from the mirror and grabbed her earrings, cell phone, and wide-brimmed hat. "Don't let those over intoxicated tenderfoots slip over the side of the boat and into the Rogue River."

Ma chuckled. "That's my job, although today we've got a crowd of Mennonites. They're treating their families and employees to a jet boat excursion to celebrate the end of harvest." She waggled her brows. "No hard-liquor-drinking customers, thank the Lord."

"Nice." She followed Ma into the kitchen. "I'll bet you're glad the season is over. Now you can paint until your eyes cross."

Ma retrieved her lunch bag and her purse. "Hmmm. My last day." She closed her eyes. "I can't wait to reorganize my studio. Snuggle in for the winter. Listen to the fire crackle in my little woodstove."

When Ma left the house, Vale worked to insert her silver earrings and thought about her ma's job as nature instructor on one of the scenic jet boat tours. Vale would rather ride horses at the stables where she worked. Ma sometimes dealt with city folks who drank too much. And about once a month, someone fell off one of the jet boats and into the white water of the Rogue River. No one had ever drowned, though. Not on Ma's watch.

Vale grabbed the keys and used her free hand to pat her French-braided hair. Smooth. Strands in place. She stuffed her hat on her head and grinned at the thought to look nice for the horses. At the door, she snapped her fingers. She hurried back and went into the kitchen. Vale swiped the brown sack off the counter and peeked inside. The savory scent of sliced whole grain bread, sprouts, and avocado made her mouth water.

She glanced at Daddy's empty coffee cup in the sink. He'd left an hour ago for his job as head manager of the local sawmill.

As the Jeep engine warmed, she called Caleb. When he didn't pick up, she left a message.

Now in first gear, she eased along their lengthy driveway. Before Vale turned onto the main road, she prayed. "Lord, God, Caleb needs this hunting trip more than I do. Please help him feel well enough so he can go. In Jesus' name I ask. Amen."

IT WAS HER job each day to groom and ride at least three of the ten horses at Wild Rogue Stables. Snickers, the paint, was the most high-spirited. Today he pawed the ground, and dust rose around his hoof. As she checked the logbook, she chuckled. "I'm sorry, Snicks, you were the last one left for the fourth day."

She saddled Snickers and rode him hard. One didn't just ride Snickers. Vale discovered long ago, he loved to gallop until her own thighs ached.

As she walked Snickers back to the corral, Princess Polly, her Polish Arabian mare whinnied. She waved. "Hey, girl." She rode over and kissed Princess on the forehead. "It's your turn next." Princess nodded her head, blowing air through her nostrils. Did she understand? Probably. The horse acted more human than animal, and no one better tell Vale otherwise.

Over the last few weeks, she had ridden Princess daily after work hours. The extra exercise prepared her horse for the rugged, high elevation deer paths to their favorite hunting sites. For the same reason, she also made time to ride Caleb's horse Storming.

Now, the trail she liked to use near the stables for Princess and Storming was overgrown. To the point she had to duck to avoid bigger branches which fingered out from the madrones and firs.

Later, back at the stall, she hugged her horse's neck. Princess nibbled at Vale's braid, and a mouthful disappeared between her teeth. She giggled. "Nuh uh." She eased the wad of wet hair free. "That's mine."

While she saddled Storming, her thoughts went to Caleb. She nibbled her lip. Three more days before she knew if he was able to take the trip.

HER EVENING SHOWER done, she had rid herself of the odor of horse and manure. Now she called Caleb.

"Yeah?" He croaked.

"Sorry, I thought you'd still be up."

"Nope."

"Long day?"

"Uh, huh."

She waited and hoped he'd wake enough to chat. "Okay, then, umm, I'll let you go."

He mumbled. "Yep."

They disconnected, and she frowned at her phone. First off, he never called her back from this morning. Second, he never went to bed before ten. She checked the time. "It's only seven, for crying out loud."

THE TWEET OF her cell phone interrupted her horse dream. She fumbled closer to the edge of the bed and snatched her phone off her nightstand. "Hello?"

"Wake up, sleepy head."

She craned her neck to check her alarm clock, but it sat in the shadows of predawn. "What time is it?"

"Almost five."

"Caaaaleb." She plopped back on the bed. "This feels too early even for the birds. Is this payback for me waking you last night?"

Silence on the other end.

"Caleb?"

"You called me?"

"Yes, silly." She yawned out. "I called at seven and you were asleep."

"Oh. Well. You woke me, so I wake you."

"Brat."

"Brat back at ya."

She squirmed and sat up against the headboard. "Why were you asleep so early?"

"Just tired, I guess. I have two more cords for Mr. McCullough, and he'll be set for the winter."

"Will it be done before we leave you think?"

It sounded as though he slurped on his coffee before he answered. "Easily."

Vale yawned again and blinked at the sleepy tears in her eyes. "Ahhhh. I've got to fix a cup of tea so I can function." She threw back the quilts and stepped across the wood floor in her stocking feet. "Man, it's cold this morning. I'll bet it's even colder your way."

"Let me check." He paused. "It's twenty-eight degrees."

"Brrr." In the kitchen, she bent to kiss her mother's and father's cheeks as they ate their breakfast. "Hi, Ma. Hi Daddy. I'm talking to Caleb." She spoke into the phone again. "This is like an early cold snap."

Jack, Vale's daddy, nodded. "Tell him hi for me, and I've been praying."

She extended her arm. "You say it, Daddy, while I start my tea."

Daddy's extra-large hand curled around the phone. "Hi, Son. I know we spoke when you returned from the hospital, but I wanted you to know I'm praying for you."

Ma said, "Let me say a few words when you're through." A while later, Daddy said his goodbyes and Ma raised her voice to a higher note. "Good morning, Caleb." She paused. "Good, good. You sound chipper, honey."

While they continued their conversation, Vale's tea had finished steeping. She added a bit of honey, stirred, and sipped on her mug with the logo *Love the Oregon*

Coast. "My turn." She accepted the phone from Ma. "Hey, Cuz, I'll feel human any second now."

"Ah, I see." He chuckled. "Green tea?"

"Of course. You know me and my daily antioxidants."

He laughed. "You're a health food freak."

She whispered, "So how are you really doing?"

"Good, good."

"Are you still planning to take physical therapy?"

"Oh, sure, when we get back from our hunting trip."

Ma mouthed, "What?"

Vale covered the phone speaker with a hand. "He's going to start therapy after our trip."

The sides of her mouth drooped, and Ma shook her head. "He should do the essential oils now like I suggested."

Caleb asked, "What'd she say?"

She stared at Ma. "Essential oils." If Caleb could see Ma's expression . . .

He sighed. "She's not happy about my medication."

"You never gave her natural remedies a chance." Vale rubbed the edge of her ear. "Honestly, Caleb, she can't help worrying."

"Yeah, I'm sure." His chuckle sounded forced. "Only herbs and spices for what ails you."

"And oils." She sauntered down the hall and into the bathroom with her mug of tea. "You've gotten the point over the years."

"Did I ever. But, seriously, Vale, I don't mean to upset Auntie."

"I know, I know. Everyone makes their choices." She thought of Papa and his supposed suicide. Was it really true? Maybe Ma was mistaken. Maybe the autopsy report got it wrong. Maybe, Vale had become delusional. Papa. The man she still loved, and who let her stand on his one hand to balance her in the air as an older baby. She even had the photo for proof.

Caleb cleared his throat. She noticed over the years it had become more of a nervous habit. "I've got to get to the woods so I can meet the sun there."

She set her mug on the bathroom counter. "See you Friday." With her free hand, she ran a brush through her hair.

"Can't wait."

Did his voice sound hollow?

She wrinkled her brows and set down her brush. "Bye." She walked out of the bathroom and tossed her cell on the couch. As she entered the kitchen, she gulped the last of the warm liquid. Daddy had his jacket and ball cap on, and kissed her on the cheek. "See you tonight, Peanut."

Snuggled in his hug, her nose squished against his woodsy-scented jacket. "Okay, Daddy."

The front door opened and shut behind him, while Vale sliced off a piece of her mom's rye bread and settled it in the toaster. When it popped up, she spread on a thick layer of butter. The view through the kitchen window at their tree-lined property was her favorite spot from the house. Most often, it calmed her. But today she couldn't stop her worry that Caleb might not be able take their trip on Friday.

Her imagination could be as wild as a herd of mustangs.

6~LEADS ME
CALEB

CALEB WRAPPED A heavy-duty chain around the last log and hooked it onto a link before he jumped into the cab. He let his hand fall from the key in the ignition as his gut churned. The instrument panel before him blurred, and he gripped the wheel. *What's happening?*

Minutes later, and many deep breaths, the symptoms left. As he reached for the ignition key again, his arm might as well have carried a log. His muscles had grown weak. *Water.* He gulped from his water jar and swiped his mouth across his sleeve.

He blinked at whirls of autumn leaves across his windshield. Caleb started to lose the eager anticipation for this time of year. Vale would be heartbroken if he decided not to go hunting. He shook his head. Not an option.

They *would* go to Papa's cabin. Besides, his head pain had lessened. But what was the deal about the dizzy spell? Would it happen again? *Please, Lord.* He became off kilter like a bear who woke grumpy from one of his long winter naps.

Kippy broke into his inward thoughts. Her bark came sharp, high-pitched. Kippy's bark told him a lot. This playful sound didn't indicate danger. Right then, his phone played the western movie theme song, The Magnificent Seven. "Hello?"

"Caleb Cutter?"

The female voice caused him to pause. He smiled. "Yes, ma'am."

"This is Doctor Roger's office. Remember me, Cherry?"

"Of course." *How could I not?* His heart pounded as though Kippy's paws danced inside his chest. *Thrummed, thrummed, thrummed.* "How-how are you?" He tried to breathe deeply but failed.

"Doing well, thank you." She hesitated. "I, ah, called to see how you are managing since your last appointment."

"Oh." The prancing within his chest eased. *Medical call.* "I'm doing okay." *Tell her about the strange spells.* He shook his head no.

Her voice had a lilt to a higher note. "That's wonderful."

He nodded at the phone.

She cleared her throat.

Not wanting to ruin the conversation with negative words, he said, "How are you?"

"Great," she breathed.

He checked his watch, and it showed a few minutes pass one o'clock. "I'll bet you're real busy."

"Lunch break."

He raised his brows. "You made this call on your own time?"

She giggled.

His lips spread into a man-sized grin.

"Caleb? Can you hear me?"

He sprang from the cab and paced. "So, this isn't really a doctor's kind of call? Like when you check on a patient?" He balled his fingers into a fist and hoped she'd say what he wanted to hear.

"I'm sorry." She made a noise in her throat. "I don't mean to pry. I just wanted to make sure you're okay." Silence for the space of three heartbeats. "Do you mind, Caleb?"

He dug the toe of his boot into the dirt. "Mind?" A chuckle rumbled in his chest. "Not a bit." Then he grew serious. "Does this mean you're nosey with all the patients?"

"Never."

He switched the cell to his other ear. "Really?"

"Honest."

His throat clogged in emotion, but he managed to speak. "Is there anything else you'd like to know about me?"

"Yes, Caleb."

As God was his Creator, he could hear a grin in her, *Yes, Caleb*. He inhaled courage and exhaled doubt. "I've got an idea on how we could get to know each other better."

"How's that?" Her voice lilt to a higher note.

"Let's meet tonight for supper at the halfway point in Myrtle Creek."

Her breath came soft through the phone. "Yes, sir, Mr. Cutter."

He pulled the phone away from his mouth, and exclaimed in a hushed whisper, "Hot diggity." His vocal cords wanted to howl like a coyote, so he cleared his throat to keep them trapped. "Okay, then. How about we meet at Great Eats & Treats? Do you know the place?"

"Yes." There went that pause, again. "Have you taken other girls there?"

Did she sound jealous? "Ah—" She caught him off guard. "Well. I'm not joking when I say this. But. I've never had a date."

Her voice raised an octave. "*Ahhh.*"

His face flushed with heat. "I'm a freak, huh?" Although she didn't sound shocked.

"No, no, Caleb. I think it's sweet."

He looked at his phone and mouthed, *Sweet?* He shook his head and chuckled. "Can you make it at six?"

"Could we make it seven? I work until six on Wednesdays."

He slapped his thigh with his ball cap. "Yes ma'am."

"See you there, Caleb."

"Wait a minute." He held out his hand. "What kind of car do you drive?"

"A red Volkswagen."

To match her hair. "I drive a blue Ford pickup."

When they disconnected, he danced a jig on the autumn leaves. Kippy pranced before him and barked and whined. "I've got a date with a ginger head, Kippy." He did the twist dance a time or two and hurried to his pickup.

Renewed gusto pushed him to work faster. He cut a log into 20-inch, woodstove-sized chunks. Hours later, he split the last log and looked around. When had the sky grown dusky? His gut rumbled. He forgot to eat lunch. Caleb packed the equipment, attached the log splitter to the hitch, and jumped into the cab. While he drove, he whistled to the song *Amazing Grace* and headed across Mr. McCullough's meadow. A doe caught his eye as she fed on meadow grass. He braked. Did a buck hide nearby? The doe veered her head to the left, and a fawn leaped from behind a Manzanita bush. Mama doe stared at Caleb, before she munched on the grass once again.

As the fawn darted to its mother, its tail flicked. Then the little guy twirled and kicked in playful abandonment.

Kippy peeked her head through the open window and barked at the deer. Both mother and fawn startled and hopped into the heavy brush.

Not a bit interested in fawns and dogs, Caleb visualized Cherry across from him in the booth at Great Eats & Treats. Would she suck on a straw buried in a chocolate, strawberry or vanilla shake? If he were to bet, he'd say strawberry. And would they laugh and joke?

Before he left the restaurant, he'd hold her hand, even if it was in a handshake.

CALEB SHOWERED LIKE a man on fire. No five-minute wash for him. Nu uh. He took it long. He took it hot. Sawdust clung, so he washed every speck of debris, sweat, and chainsaw-slinging reside from his tanned skin. As he showered, he sang in a holler, *Jesus Loves Me.*

Afterward, he dressed in a hurry. Black shirt with preacher collar, boot-cut jeans, and his newer square-toed cowboy boots. Nana's grandfather clock chimed six times. He stuffed his wallet in his back pocket and headed for the front door. His dog raced past him through the doorway and across the swinging bridge. Caleb's command came sharp. "Kippy. Get back inside."

Head lowered, she turned and slinked toward the cottage. Before he locked her inside, she peered at him and pulled a face. Real slow, she *blink, blink, blink*ed.

"Now, stop. I'm going on my first date, Kip, and you can't come." When he returned, he'd for sure find her asleep on his bed. That is, if he snuck in quiet-like and caught her not in her own bed at the foot of his mattress on the floor.

Caleb drove too fast down the mountain. He didn't notice the lights on inside homes of the farms and ranches he passed as he normally would. His thoughts were only on a single person. Cherry. At the thought of her name, his palms became sweaty where they gripped the wheel. What do you say to a lady on the first date? He had no practice. Zero. Not a thing to guide him from a past success. Maybe Vale was correct. He should have dated a few girls before he met the one he was drawn to. Would this be his only chance to make an impression?

Would he blow it?

Then again, Papa always stressed to wait for that special lady. So Caleb had waited. If Cherry was not for him, who cared if he blew it? He gripped the steering wheel. But he did care, and he didn't know why.

As he pulled onto the Interstate, he decided to stop at Rolly's Market in Canyondale and buy flowers. He'd have to make it quick, though. When he arrived, he searched for red ones in the potted flowers display. A sudden dizzy spell slammed into him, and he leaned into a shelf while moisture collected above his upper lip.

"Sir?" A woman's voice spoke near him. "May I help you?"

He glanced at a silver-haired lady and wiped at his mouth. "Do you have any red roses?"

"Come this way." She waved her fingers for him to follow. "We keep our cut flowers in the cooler."

At the other end of the store, the lady stopped in front of a refrigerated flower case. "Do you see anything you like?" Her eyes crinkled as though she was eager to help.

He spotted a small bouquet of six red roses, baby's breath, and ferns. He pointed to them. "I'll take those."

Back in the pickup, his body tensed, and his mind filled with dread. Would Cherry like him? Or would she be sorry about the date? He shook his head. Where did that come from?

When he pulled into the Great Eats & Treats parking lot, he sat in the pickup and checked every car. A chill snaked along his spine. Is this what it felt like to get cold feet? He could always leave early. Caleb closed his eyes and prayed for courage. To relax.

A tap, tap sounded on his window. Cherry. Her smile. A wave. His fears melted like snow on a warm spring day.

IN THE RESTAURANT, Cherry sipped her strawberry shake through a straw. "I know what you mean, Caleb." The bouquet of flowers sat on the table next to her.

They discussed the problem of poachers. That they killed game out of season. Especially the slaughter of whole herds of bull elk, and the poachers left the meat to rot. He wiped his sweaty palms across his thighs. She frowned. "Are you okay?"

"Sure." *Not even.* The room whipped around him again. *Lord.* A groan traveled toward his throat, but he pursed his lips.

"You seem agitated." She pointed at his empty platter. "You ate well."

He ignored her question and asked her to tell him about her favorite foods. As he listened, he had an urge to touch her around the mouth. Unlike most women, Cherry wore no makeup. She didn't need any.

How could he have considered cutting the date short? She acted sweet, a soft-spoken, real lady. If it weren't for his idiotic spells, it would be the perfect night. Thank goodness the dizziness was going away. He continued to study her. Did Cherry always smile this much on a date? She slumped a bit, her hands on her lap.

He relaxed. "Tell me about your work."

She leaned closer. "I'm blessed to have such a great job. I try to understand that people most often wait until they feel really sick, then they panic and call." Cherry folded her hands on top of the table. "I also take a few online classes at the college. Do you attend school in Southern Oregon?"

"No." He angled his head. "I'm a woodsman. I'll take the mountains any day over a study book. But I'm in the process of becoming an official hunting guide, because I enjoy the slopes and the meat is a big draw. I've already taken some friends the last few seasons, and they almost always get their game."

As she spoke of her family life, he grew mesmerized. He'd stepped into another world where all was calm, and all was right. The night's conversation would have continued, until he checked his watch. "We've talked for almost three hours."

The waitress came again for the umpteenth time. "Is there anything else I can get you kids?"

They exchanged a glance, and they both shook their heads.

"I'll get your bill, hon." She made a beeline for the register.

He arched his brow at Cherry and mouthed *hon.* Her hand covered her mouth, and she giggled. He leaned closer. "You wanna share a piece of their dark chocolate cake?"

She waved her arms as though she threw caution to the mountaintops. "Let's pig out."

Oh, how he liked her even more. A daring lady.

When the waitress returned, he pointed at the dessert menu. "We've decided to share a piece of your chocolate cake." He smiled. "If it's not time to close."

The waitress wrote on their ticket. "I think you have time for cake." She winked. "I'll return in a jiffy."

While they waited, Caleb wondered how it would feel to touch Cherry's ginger hair. And, her skin held a soft glow, and he'd bet his last dollar it would be silky.

She placed her hands over her stomach. "I can't remember the last time I ate this much." She leaned closer. "I have to confess that when I'm happy I tend to eat more."

She was happy? Did she like him? He remembered his earlier dare to touch her fingers. "Oh, I'm a hog when it comes to chocolate." His arms reached across the table, and he gently pressed her fingers.

Her cheeks pinked to a soft blush as their eyes held in an unbroken gaze. The waitress set the slice of cake with two forks between them. "Do you kids need an extra plate?" They shook their heads no. "Didn't think so." She walked away to the front door window and flipped the Open sign to Closed.

Caleb sliced off a piece of the cake and reached toward Cherry's mouth. She blinked as though surprised and opened her mouth to eat the bite. Her cheeks grew crimson, and she squirmed in her chair. He sensed she may be embarrassment and handed her the other fork.

They ate the rest of their cake in silence. Did he offend her? He should have not fed her the piece of cake on their first date. When he motioned for her to eat the last piece, Cherry wiped her lips with a napkin. "I'm stuffed, Caleb, and I better go. It's late."

"Yep, it's ten."

She stood, and he paid the waitress. Outside, he opened her car door. She slid onto the seat and started the engine. He wanted to hang out until midnight. Stare at her. Memorize every freckle, bask in the single mole near her upper lip, and soak in her light brown eyes. The car door shut instead. Maybe she felt the same, because she rolled down the window and grinned.

Caleb slapped the door frame. "I'll call you tomorrow?"

She nodded, and her eyes held a gleam.

His sigh came quick, so relieved he hadn't upset her about feeding her cake. "When do you leave for work?"

She blinked. "Eight."

He stuffed his hands in his pockets. "I'll call before eight, then. If it's okay."

"I'd like that, Caleb."

"I'm going on a bow hunting trip in two days with my cousin, Vale. We'll be gone for a week."

"Nice." She drew closer and crossed her arms on the window frame. "Where at?"

He waved a hand toward the northwest. "In the coastal range near Powers. We always stay in our papa's cabin."

She tapped her fingers on her other arm. "Sounds like fun." She waved. "Goodbye, Caleb, and thank you for the beautiful roses."

He winked. "Thank you for accepting my invitation to dinner."

As she backed out and drove through the parking lot, her taillights flickered. Was she waving another goodbye? An idea came to him. They'd spend more time together sooner than later.

That is if she agreed.

7~IN THE PATHS
VALE

"ARE YOU SERIOUS?" She hollered into her phone as she tugged on the lead rope of one stubborn mule, Sprinkles, a new arrival at the horse stables. In disgust, she shook her head at both Caleb's how-dare-he words and the equine's behavior. "You know I can't talk right now."

She cut off their conversation and stuffed the phone in her vest pocket. "Some nerve." She nudged the rope, and this time Sprinkles walked alongside Vale. "You better behave, Miss Sassy Pants. I'm not in the mood to mess around, especially after that call." The mule snorted and shook her head up and down as if in rebellion. Vale stared right back at Sprinkles' eye. "I don't need you to give me fits." Her nerves buzzed as though coffee induced, but she'd switched to tea long ago.

As they strolled around the pen, she spoke to the horse. "Since when do we have an outsider at Papa's cabin? Never. That's when." For eleven years, they went up to the cabin during deer season with their papa. At first the cousins carried only binoculars and a pocket knife and scoped for deer. When they were old enough to receive their license, they hunted.

During the first two years, Papa taught the distinction between doe and buck tracks. What buck scat looked like verses doe scat, although even the professional hunters argued amongst themselves, saying that was a myth. The cousins took their papa's word for it that they could know the difference. Another thing important to Papa was how to walk in the woods and what to wear on their feet. He bought them a well-made brand of moccasins with sturdy leather. Much quieter than boots or tennis shoes.

But Papa was gone and then Caleb's call. "He's going to ruin our birthday hunting trip."

Her boss, Wynonna Wilder met her at the entrance of the tack room. "Talking to the animals?"

"Yep."

"You look agitated." Wynonna stared at her. "I've got five minutes to listen before I head over to Winston to see about an Arabian mare."

Vale guided Sprinkles closer to the saddle stand and tied her halter straps to a rail. She placed a blanket on the mule's back. "Right now, I'm angry at my cousin." As she grasped both ends of the saddle, she lifted and then settled the saddle on Sprinkle's blanket.

Her boss crossed her arms. "Ah ha. Caleb." She leaned her jean-clad hip against the wall. "I'm listening."

She shook her head, one wag each way. "I can't believe what he just suggested. We always went to Papa's cabin, just the two of us and Papa. But you know Papa's gone." She bent and cinched the saddle but not too tight. "Now Caleb called and had the nerve to say he's met a girl."

Wynonna shifted her boots on the concrete. "Oh?"

She stood and gazed at Wynonna. "This is a real problem."

Her bosses eyes grew soft. "I can see."

Vale stepped close to Sprinkles and buckled the second belt under her, closer to her hind legs. "He wants to invite—" she tugged the belt with a grunt— "a stranger for opening weekend of bow hunt."

"So, he hasn't actually made the invitation."

Tears stung behind the bridge of Vale's nose. "He better not."

"What did you tell him?"

In a jerk motion, she snugly tightened the first cinch. "I'd call him back."

"I'm sorry, kiddo." Wynonna tapped her watch. "I've got that appointment. Keep talking to Sprinkles. Let me know what you decide."

"Okay."

Wynonna strode from the tack room.

Vale checked the mule's bridle and grew even sulkier. "You're lucky, Sprinkles." She stuck her boot in the stirrup, sat, and settled her other boot in second stirrup. She clicked her tongue for the mule to walk on. "You don't have to deal with surprises." Maybe that wasn't entirely true. She figured Sprinkles would get bit or kicked before the other horses accepted her into their herd.

Alone on the trail, she thought out loud to help sort through things. "Sprinkles, am I being too selfish with Caleb? He has been having a tough time, and he's never had a girlfriend." Cotton-ball clouds contrasted against the blue sky. "Well, except for that girl, Hope, in fourth grade and that didn't count. They were just kids." *But, Lord, he has me, his best friend.*

She rode in silence for a while, and then broke the quiet. "Sprinkles, what would Jesus do?" They approached a cleared area dotted with short weeds. Down the middle, a path was worn by the horses. At the click of her tongue, she dug in her heels. The mule galloped, and the breeze flowed over Vale's face. Soon, they both were winded, and she slowed to a walk. "So,

Sprinkles, maybe this friend of Caleb's just wants to be at the cabin and not go hunting. We only have two horses, anyway." Wait. Did he think she'd let a stranger ride her horse? *Surely not!*

At the one-mile marker, she clicked her tongue again and tapped her boot heels into Sprinkles' side. She took the horse into an extended trot through a meadow. Finally, she reined in a little for a walk as she patted the mule on the neck. "You're a good listener, Sprinkles." The mule blew through her nostrils as though she agreed.

Vale spotted the stables, then speed dialed Caleb's number. "Hey, it's me. It's okay if you want to bring what's-her-name."

"It's Cherry Danube. And thanks, Vale."

She shrugged. "I didn't like it at first, but you and I still get five days to hunt." She sucked in a breath. "Wait. She doesn't want to hunt, does she?"

"I don't know. I'll ask her about hunting or if she just wants to go horseback riding. If she decides to accept my offer to spend Friday night and all day Saturday."

"But on whose horse?"

Silence at Caleb's end. Then, "Well, that is something I hadn't considered."

"A third horse means we'd have to borrow or rent a bigger trailer." When he said nothing, she thought to let that part go. For now. The mule stumbled, and she hung on to the saddle horn. "I'm glad you didn't just go and invite her without asking me."

"That would be rude."

"Let me know what she says."

"Sure will."

She'd disconnected the call, and Vale scratched Sprinkles on the shoulder. "I hope this Cherry person isn't a tenderfoot of irritation."

IN HER BEDROOM, Vale browsed over her list for the umpteenth time. She sat on her bed next to Tootsie, her gray cat. "Poison oak soap. Check. Toothpaste. Check. Toothbrush. Check." A sigh escaped between her lips. Truth be told, she did not want Cherry along and never on opening day. She flopped on her bed. "I'm jealous, Tootsie. Plain and simple." Jealous emotions were never simple. It could tear people apart. She knew this from public school.

But how could he think this wouldn't bother her? She grabbed her spiral notebook and flung it hard. It hit the wall and plopped on the floor, pages fluttered and closed.

A knock came on the door. "Vale?"

She crossed her arms and fought tears.

The door opened, and Ma peeked in. "What's all the noise?"

"I threw my notebook," she mumbled, "because I'm angry." She faced Ma and jutted her chin. "Caleb invited this girl he just met to go with us to Papa's cabin for the weekend." She spread her fingers and shook her hands in front of her. "She'll ruin everything."

Ma folded her hands at her waist. "You don't know for sure if she's going?"

"No." She bent, snagged her notebook off the floor, and sat on the edge of the bed. Vale curled her arms over the notebook as though cardboard and paper could give her comfort.

Ma settled next to her, and their knees touched. "But if this makes Caleb happy—"

Vale cut her a look.

"Honey, you're being too possessive."

She relaxed her neck back and noticed the cobwebs on her ceiling. "I know."

"You're not children anymore."

"I still remember how lost and sad he was when he came to live with us after Aunty Lynn and Uncle Brad died."

"About that." Ma touched her hand. "I was so glad you made it your mission to make him feel loved and accepted." Ma gave her an even stare. "But, honey, you'll each make your own way very soon. Maybe this weekend will be the start. And, sweetheart, we all miss Papa."

With a jerk, she wagged her head. "What does that have to do with this?"

"Plenty."

Vale's muscle's tensed as she grew impatient for her mother's explanation.

"Listen to me, honey. This year your papa will be absent. That's hard for you both." Ma spread out her arms. "Maybe, for Caleb, he needs a third person even if it's someone he's just met. Then, maybe, it won't hurt so much in Papa's absence."

"But what about me?" Tears stung behind the bridge of her nose. "I miss Papa too."

"Hear me out, Vale." She waved her hand. "I think for you, your way to grieve for Papa's absence is to have Caleb all to yourself." Ma's gentle smile seemed to soften her bold words. "Am I right?"

"Well." She fluttered her lashes and cleared her blurry vision. "Maybe. But still, I'm so not ready for Caleb and me to go our own ways, Ma."

"See what I mean, honey? On the heels of your papa's death, maybe you can't handle what you feel as losing Caleb also. For there to be someone special in his life other than you." Ma draped an arm around Vale's shoulders. "I suppose you're not ready, but it seems Caleb is ahead of you in that department."

"Too bad for me." She reached for the box of tissue on her dresser, lifted two layers, and blew her nose into the cushiony softness. The two kept silent for long moments, until she thought of what Ma said about Papa. "Thank you for mentioning Papa and about us missing him. No one mentions his name anymore."

"You're welcome, honey, and you're right." Ma bent forward. "I'll do better from now on to talk about my dad."

On a perfect toss, Vale's crinkled tissue landed inside her waste basket. "You should have heard Caleb's voice go all gooey when he spoke about Cherry." She rolled her eyes to the cobwebbed ceiling. "Brother."

Ma chuckled. "I can't seem to get you to think about something else."

"Believe me, he's bombed over her." She snapped her fingers. "You know what's bugging me?" Ma shook her head. "Caleb sounds so head over heels for her, and they just met, for crying out loud."

Ma rested her arms on her lap and intertwined her fingers. "Sometimes these things happen fast. Maybe it will for him."

"Please, don't even go there." She could just see it. Caleb married in a matter of months, maybe in the spring. She groaned.

"You must accept it could happen, honey. For your relationship's sake, you must."

Vale bowed her head and stared at the cookie crumbs on her blue carpet.

Ma continued. "I remember a certain little girl in fourth grade that he kissed. Remember? You wouldn't speak to him for the rest of the day."

She glanced at Ma. "I thought of Hope." Vale snatched a flyswatter from her nightstand. "I think she was jealous of my and Caleb's relationship." She stood. On tiptoes, she dragged the swatter over the cobwebs near the ceiling. "I saw the tip of her tongue more than a few times."

Ma laughed. "Did you tell him?"

"I did, and he didn't believe me." She walked along her room and scraped down a few more webs. "What if Cherry doesn't like me?" She twisted to face Ma.

"That, my dear," Ma tapped her own chin, "would be uncomfortable for the three of you."

"You can say that again." She paced in her room. "This is too sudden. We need to meet first." She halted her steps. "Does that make sense?"

"Sure, honey." Ma moved to stand in front of Vale and squeezed her shoulders.

She kissed her mother's cheek. "Thanks, Mama."

Ma closed the door behind her, and Vale pressed Caleb's name on her phone. He answered, "Hey."

"Have you asked Cherry yet?"

He chuckled. "You never have been one to beat around the blackberry bushes. Yes. We just got off the phone, and she'll meet me at the freeway exit. She will follow me to my cottage where we can meet you. From there, we'll go to Papa's cabin."

Vale's good intentions vanished on her next breath. "Oh." She pursed her lips.

"Do I hear disappointment in your *oh*?"

She scratched an itch on her scalp. "Well—it does complicate things."

"How do you figure?"

"Do we bring three horses?" She raised her voice. "We'll need more food. Just to name a few."

"She doesn't ride, I already asked." He hesitated. "Or I could teach her."

Vale pulled the phone from near her mouth and raised her chin to the ceiling. "Please, deliver me." She heaved a breath and blew air through her nose. "Come on, Caleb. This sounds like a babysitting job."

"Whoa, calm down."

"You're the one who changed our plans. Not me."

"Valie, Valie."

She snarled. "What?" She raised her hand to throw the phone across the room. But froze.

". . . a night and one day."

Her lips quivered. "Is there any way I can meet her before Friday?"

"Let's just leave it as is, shall we? Besides, you're going to like her."

She debated whether she should argue.

"Valie, you there?" He chuckled. "You know I love you best and always will."

"No, you won't. Ma's right, one day you'll go your way, and I'll go mine. You'll get married. I'll get married."

"That's what people do, Valie, and we'll always be close." Caleb *tsk*ed his tongue. "We'll raise our kids together. Don't you see?"

Her back stiffened. "I can't seem to help myself. I feel scared I'll lose you when you have friends who are girls."

"You finally admit it."

"I do." She nodded. "And I'm sorry. But I won't promise to stop being jealous this very exact moment."

"Haven't I been nice to your guy friends?"

Was that a grin within his words? "Yes, you have."

"Come on, Vale." He sighed. "I want you to be willing to get to know Cherry. Just give her a chance."

"I'll try."

"Honest?" His voice raised an octave.

"I give my word."

"Good."

She nibbled at a nail on her finger. When she pulled the aggravating sharp-edged nail off, she smoothed a strand of hair from her cheek. "You may catch the love bug, you know."

"She does make me feel goose bumpy."

"I figured."

"Now Vale—"

"You're right Caleb, you're always right."

He cleared his throat. "I'm not."

"Are too."

"Am not."

Vale snickered. "Let's not argue."

"You're right."

They both laughed.

"Okay, I'm pretty much ready to share you."

"Oh, gee, thanks."

"And I'll give her a chance. For your sake." Her call waiting buzzed. "Gotta go. My boss is on the other line."

"Okay."

"Bye." She pressed the screen. "Hi, Wynonna."

"Hi, Vale. How did Sprinkles do today?"

"Great. She behaves well, and I told her she fits right in at Nonna Stables."

"Oh?" Wynonna chuckled. "What did she say?"

"She nickered her agreement. Great listener, that mule."

"This, my dear, is all horses and mules. We should save ourselves the therapist fees and talk to horses." She paused. "When you come in tomorrow, I'll be gone." The tone of her voice meant the talk had turned to business. "Would you shovel and disinfect the stalls? Only exercise a horse or two if there is time."

Vale angled her face away from the phone and blew her nose on a tissue.

Wynonna explained. "I've got an inspection on Monday. We need to keep our status as a topnotch boarding facility."

"What will you do about the cleanup on Monday? I won't be there."

She puffed out a breath. "I know you'll be gone. I'll go in a couple hours early and shovel what little bit of manure is in the stalls. At least the stalls will be scrubbed good tomorrow."

"If I finish, may I leave sooner?"

"You sound stuffy. Do you have a cold?"

"No, I've—been upset."

"Is this over Caleb's visitor?"

Vale cleared her throat. "Yes, and I'm trying to adjust to him bringing his friend."

"You need to talk to Sprinkles again."

"Better God than a mule at this point. I struggle here, even though I told him I would give Cherry a chance."

"I hear ya, kiddo. What's up about you wanting to leave early?"

"Caleb's new friend makes one more mouth to feed. I need to shop for a few extras before we leave on Friday."

"Okay, hon. Do you need a larger horse trailer?"

"Well, no. Caleb wants to teach her to ride, so I've decided to loan her Princess."

"That's good because I need mine for Saturday. My kids and I will be on a trail ride at Crater Lake."

"Sounds fun." Vale yawned. "Sorry. I'm beat."

"No need to apologize. Okay, Vale, you guys have a great week, and I'll see you when you get back."

Vale ended the call and stared in the mirror and over her shoulder. Pictures of Caleb and her plastered the wall. He *was* her best friend. And a friend must always be kind. She'd be nice this weekend. For Caleb's sake.

THE NEXT DAY, Vale shut the outer stable door which led into the pasture so a horse couldn't come back inside. Then, she shoveled out manure from each stall and into a large wheelbarrow. She hauled twenty loads to a pile at the end of the stables. Later, she'd call people on the list who bought manure for their gardens.

At one o'clock, she scraped her boot heels on the brushes attached to a board. As she washed her hands and face in the tiny bathroom sink in the stables, her cell phone chimed. She glanced at the screen. Caleb.

8~OF RIGHTEOUSNESS
CALEB

HE WANDERED INTO the bathroom to finish packing his shaving kit. Before he knew what was happening, his vision blurred and his stomach blurped. *Nausea.* He sat on the side of the tub, but it went on too long. He pressed the speed dial, and his fingers trembled.

"Hey, Caleb."

His breath came ragged. "Where are you?"

She gasped. "You sound sick."

"Can't catch my breath. Feel like I'm going to crawl out of my skin."

"Oh. No. Has it happened before?"

"Yeah, but this time it's worse."

"How long ago did it start?"

Sweat trickled along his neck. "A few days ago, but it wasn't this bad." Caleb coughed and pressed a hand to his chest. Would his heart race right out of his chest?

"Are you lying down?" Her voice shook.

"Nuh-uh."

"Get prone and prop your head on two pillows."

He moved to Nana's sofa, stacked two throw pillows at one end, and lay down. "I'm on the sofa."

"Now, I'm praying."

He nodded to himself.

"Lord, please lay Your calming Spirit over Caleb. Whatever this is, please stop it. In Jesus' name I ask. Amen."

Calm did flow through him. It was so much better when someone else prayed.

"Are you there?"

"Thanks, Vale." His voice became whisper soft. "Just what I needed."

"Now, don't laugh, Cuz, but you need to take a hot salts bath."

"That's for girls."

"C'mon, Caleb. It'll help your body relax."

"Another one of Auntie's remedies?"

"Yes. There should be salts under your bathroom sink, because Papa used it to soak his feet. Get rested for tomorrow. I'll be there— ah, I mean, if you still feel able to make the trip."

"I will." *I better anyway.* His head had stopped its insane whirl, and he entered the bathroom and found the salts. "What would I do without your organizational skills?"

"Be unorganized."

"Ha. Sure." He turned on the faucets to fill the tub and shook out about a cup of the salts.

"How are you feeling now?"

"A bit better. A hot soak does sound like a good thing, especially in this big claw-foot tub." Several breaths later, he said, "But you better not tell anyone I'm soaking in lavender salts. Like a girl."

"Papa got lavender scented?" She chuckled. "I won't tell. Good night, Caleb, and I'll see you—"

"Tomorrow." *I hope.*

The long soak soothed him, and he dried off and sniffed. He smelled like a girl, but he didn't care as he crawled into bed exhausted. He thanked God for his family and had almost fallen asleep when doubts attacked. He hoped he'd be fit enough for the hunting trip. Then, a sensation of ice slid along his spine. Was this what it felt like to experience deep-down fear? That he would never be the same after the fall on the mountain?

THE LAST OF the wood order sat in old man McCullough's shed. Exactly seven cords. Two split sixteen inches in length and five split twenty inches. Caleb drove around into the yard as Frisbee, Mr. McCullough's Jack Russell Terrier, greeted him. "Hey, girl, had any good treats lately?" He felt around in his pocket and retrieved a dog biscuit. "Catch!" Frisbee leaped five feet. She caught the biscuit in her jaws. A true acrobat. She hit the ground on all fours. "Smart dog."

Kippy barked beside him from inside the cab of the pickup, and he opened the door to let her run. The two dogs chased each other around the yard as he knocked on the old man's screened-in porch door. The door opened on screechy hinges, and a big hand caught him on the shoulder. "Hey, young Cutter. How's life treatin' ya?"

"Good, sir." *Tired.* Extra coffee for energy. Blurry vision at times. *Queasy.* Everything he ate upset his gut.

"Get in here and let's have a sit down." His steel grip attached on Caleb's arm. "Do you want a cup of coffee?"

"No, thank you, sir." He tugged off his hat and followed the old man through his older-than-dirt house. The floorboard creaked. His wife passed on a few years ago, and the old man lived in clutter and dust. When they entered the backyard, Caleb paused. A speckled fawn stretched its neck to eat a choice rose from a bush. "You have a pet, sir."

"My wife had a soft heart." Mr. McCullough sighed, a smile quivered on his lips. "She made pets of the deer years ago. Ever since then, generations of does and fawns have come here to eat the roses." He winked. "I've even caught a buck or two munching away." He raised his hands. "And Lord have mercy on my soul if I dared make one of her bucks table food."

Caleb moved to the patio set. "That's real nice, sir." The fawn jerked its head and stared at them.

The old man pulled out a chair. "Have a seat, young Cutter." The old man settled into his own chair, his aged, hairy hand slid an envelope from his tattered shirt pocket and to Caleb's side of the patio table. "Here's your earnings. I like how neat you stack my wood, son. Split just the way I like it, too, smaller and larger chunks." He nodded at Caleb. "Not too many woodcutters would split two different sizes." The old man scrubbed his meaty hand over the gray stubble on his jaw.

Caleb stashed the envelope of one-hundred-dollar bills like he always did—inside his jacket pocket. "It's my duty to make my customers happy." He knew without looking all his pay would be there, and a sizeable tip for doing the extra work to please Mr. McCullough. "I'd do the same for myself if I had two different sizes of stoves."

"Well, that's a story." The old man chuckled. "Years ago, my wife Franny just had to have this cute little enamel woodstove she found in a magazine. 'For our bedroom, Henry,' she said." He shook his head and chuckled some more. "I couldn't say no, seeing how our bedroom is so large and off the main part of the house." He leaned forward. "She had cold feet, you know."

Caleb knew, because he heard the same tale this time every year. Now his fingers danced around the brim of his hat. "I'd do the same if I had a wife." Right then his head spun, and Caleb rustled to his feet. "I should go, sir."

The old man hunched over and pushed himself up and grunted, his knees pop, pop, popped as he stood. "By the way, young Cutter, are ya ready for the buck hunt season?"

He grinned. "Sure am. Vale and I are going like we always do, even though Papa is gone."

"Up to your papa's cabin, then?" Mr. McCullough's eyes softened. "You know, your papa, Frank, and I were best friends. Our mamas were best friends. My mom told me we met at my birth, when he was six months. Our moms used to place us in the same crib for our naps while they visited." He sucked air through his teeth. "When we were tykes, I thought he was my brother." He muttered. "Might as well have been for how close we were."

When Caleb reached the front door, the old man told him he missed Frank. His fingers froze on the knob. "I do too, sir, more than I can say."

The two men, one young, one old, stared into each other's eyes. They nodded.

Mr. McCullough reached out a hand and Caleb shook it. "You kids be careful. I hope it rains for ya, so the bucks won't hear ya comin'."

On the porch, he tipped his hat. "If we get our game, sir, I'll bring you a few steaks."

The old man slapped Caleb on the back, and he dug in his heels so he wouldn't stumble. "That'd be nice, son. Did you get your bear tag?"

On the last porch step, Caleb twisted to face him. "Yes, Vale and I both did."

Mr. McCullough jabbed a finger Caleb's way. "Now that's some delicious salami. Just mix it in venison burger to tone down the flavor. Although I never did." He winked. "Give it to me bear strong."

"Yes, sir." He whistled for Kippy, and then waved goodbye to his papa's old friend. At his pickup he slid onto the leather seat and started the engine. The clock showed three p.m. He knew Vale would be at the cottage at seven o'clock sharp. He still needed to finish packing his suitcase and take a shower.

Cherry. His heart pranced. This made his chest hurt. The irregular beats continued. He should call Kippy again, since she hadn't responded. His mind grew fuzzy. He dipped his chin to his chest, and when he looked at the dash clock, too many minutes had passed. He couldn't remember anything from the past ten minutes.

As he leaned against the pickup headrest, he blew the air from his lungs. "What's happening to me?"

He didn't dare drive until he gained control, and he still needed Kippy. Caleb whistled through the open window but it sounded muffled from his weak state. His eyes scanned the meadow and beyond the tree line. A figure emerged. It was a fawn, and it jumped and wiggled its way to the stream which divided the meadow. The little fawn stopped, looked back, and flicked its tail. When the mother drew closer, the fawn twirled and ran from her. Was it the same fawn in Mr. McCullough's back yard?

Kippy appeared in a frenzied bark. She headed straight for the fawn and scared them both into the woods. Caleb whistled, and Kippy twisted and raced toward the vehicle. She soared over the tailgate and into the bed.

He pulled onto the main road. A ginger-haired lady materialized in his mind. He couldn't wait to learn more about her, and he'd have a whole day and a half to see if they might be a fit.

He had one need. Caleb hoped and prayed he didn't have any spells while Cherry visited.

CHERRY'S VEHICLE SAT on the shoulder of the road, and he eased his pickup next to her. "Follow me, mi lady." She grinned and nodded. Long minutes passed as they drove, until he pulled into his driveway. Vale's horse trailer came into view first.

He got out of the pickup and unloaded his wood cutting equipment. "Well, Cherry, are you ready for a mountain top experience?"

"I am so excited." Both her hands covered her cheeks. "I've never been to a cabin."

"It's rustic and built with logs cut from trees Papa and his daddy felled and trimmed." After he put away his tools, he touched her elbow and guided her to where the ground stopped and a bridge began.

She stiffened. "It swings?"

He tilted his head and peered at her. "Safe as can be."

As they stepped onto the wooden planks, the bridge moved. Cherry held onto the logging cable rail and squealed. "Too scary."

He tugged on her arm.

She curled in her shoulders. "Ahhh, no, no, I'll fall."

"Stay with me or you really will fall." He drew his arm around her shoulder.

Her head jerked, and she flashed him a mock glare. "You're a brut, Mr. Cutter."

"I try. I really do." They both chuckled.

Vale waved from the front door. "Hey, what's taking so long?"

"That's Vale."

Cherry's eyes brightened, and she waved back. "This bridge isn't so bad." She flashed him a one-sided grin.

He liked this lady for her attempt at bravery. And that she trusted him.

They came to the other side of the bridge where Vale waited, hands on hips. Cherry hopped to solid ground. "Whew."

Whew was right, because his head spun a little.

Cherry's face flushed, she held out a slender, pale hand. "Thank you for allowing me to barge in on part of your weekend, Vale."

Vale stared at her. "So glad to have you, Cherry." She accepted the shake. "I hope you enjoy Papa's cabin as much as we do. Nana knew how to decorate, and decorate she did. It's now our hunting lodge." She punched Caleb on the upper arm. "Right?"

He rubbed the spot. "Ow."

Vale smirked. "Let's finish loading. The bow cases are already in the Jeep."

They followed her to the porch, where Caleb had stacked his suitcase and duffle bag. He stepped into the house. "Let me grab a couple of things, and I'll be ready." As he walked inside, he reached over the door and lifted Papa's rifle and the shotgun off their racks. He grabbed the gun cleaning kit, just in case he needed it.

He grew dizzy again and leaned against the wall and waited until he regained his equilibrium. When the room stood still, he checked that lights were off and windows locked.

Vale and Cherry had already crossed the bridge, and he took the bridge a bit slower. The dizzy spell had sent waves of nausea rolling through his gut.

Once on the other side, Caleb heaved his belongings into the backseat of the Jeep. "Let's go."

Cherry moved toward her car.

He stared as she walked away. "You're not going with us?"

"Oh, no." She waved a hand at him. "This way you won't have to bring me back here when it's time for me to leave tomorrow."

He gave her the thumbs up. "Makes sense."

While Vale drove, he watched his side mirror from time to time to make sure they didn't lose Cherry. Even though he grew excited, he was also aware it could be a rough weekend. If he had anymore spells or if Vale and Cherry didn't hit it off. *Here we go, Lord.*

9~FOR HIS SAKE
VALE

AT THE CABIN, they unpacked the Jeep, and Vale hauled a box of groceries inside. Back outside, she unloaded the horses and led them to the small barn near the creek. She gave them liberal amounts of hay and oats and patted their backs. Vale spoke near Princess' ear. "Cherry will learn to ride you tomorrow. So, Princess, be nice to our beginner."

Princess stared at her owner, blinked, and returned to munch on the food. Vale closed her eyes, kissed the horse on her muzzle, and inhaled her scent. "Of course you will. You're my girl." Princess nodded her head and blew through her nose as though in agreement.

The first drops of rain pelted her as she shut the barn door and latched it against the wild creatures. She fast-walked toward the cabin and began a weekend of the unknown. But she stalled at the open front door.

"No, you don't, Caleb." Cherry's voice squeaked.

"We've just met so how would you know?"

Vale shut the door behind her and slipped off her boots. Inside the kitchen she stopped on the other side of the entryway. The two lovebirds sat at the table with glasses before them of what looked like water. "Know what?"

"I told Cherry I can eat more habanero peppers on a piece of sausage than anyone."

"He can." Vale puffed her cheeks and crossed her eyes. The idea of all those peppers was enough to make her sick. "Believe me. He's been doing it for years." She opened the refrigerator and pulled out the orange juice. "Ever since he was this tall." She raised a hand to her shoulder and poured juice into a small glass.

"Pepperoncinis are as hot as I can stomach." Cherry touched her throat. "And I wouldn't dare touch one taste bud of my tongue on a habanero."

Vale stuffed down a snort. Of course. She was too girly-girly for hot peppers. Or maybe Cherry was simply ladylike. Vale could never be one of those, though. Tomboy to the bone.

It was time to get busy. She added crushed newspaper and softwood sticks for a fire in the cookstove's firebox. When she got it to blaze and added denser wood, she filled the water-kettle and set it on the cast iron surface. In the background, the lovebirds still discussed hot peppers. She rolled her eyes heavenward. Of all the unromantic . . ... She wiggled out of her jacket and hung it on the coat hook next to the kitchen entryway. "Anyone want cocoa or hot tea?"

"I want the usual." Caleb pushed his chair back and stood.

Cherry raised a hand. Vale turned back to the stove to hide a grin. "Which is it, Cherry?"

"I'll take tea." She sidled next to Vale. "May I help?"

"There's not much to making a hot drink." Although later she could use her help to prepare supper. "Why don't you browse through the cupboards? That way I don't have to tell you where everything is when we begin our meal."

She seemed to freeze like a deer in headlights.

"Something wrong?" Vale held up a scoop of cocoa for Caleb's mug.

"Only, if you're sure."

"I only say what I mean."

Her cheeks flushed pink. "That it's not being nosy, I mean."

"Come on, Cherry, that's silly."

Caleb came behind Cherry. "What Vale means is we want you to get comfortable." He grinned. "Right, cousin?"

"Course." She controlled another eye roll and added hot water into the three mugs. She brought down the basket of teas. "This assortment of teas should be in a jar or tin." She studied Cherry. "They're from last year, so check for mice nibbles on the packets."

Cherry squealed and then slapped a hand over her mouth. She blinked as her pink fingernails flipped through the teas until she lifted a peppermint. She brought it closer to her face and examined the front of the packet and the back of the packet.

Did she check for mice holes? Vale choked down a chuckle.

Both Caleb and Cherry glanced her way.

Steaming mugs in hand, they each took a spot in the living room by the rock fireplace. The crackling fire Caleb had started earlier extended its warmth. Vale's taut muscles began to relax.

"This fireplace is huge." Cherry sipped at her tea and glanced at the cousins. "I don't think I've ever seen one take half of a wall before."

"Our papa built it." Caleb slurped on his cocoa. "He built this whole place before he married Nana, and they raised their two kids here."

She waggled a finger between Caleb and Vale. "So, two children?"

Vale pointed at her chest, "My mom," she pointed at him, "and his dad are siblings."

He took another gulp of his drink. "But my parents were killed in a car wreck when I was ten. Vale's mom and dad adopted me."

Cherry nodded and blew on her tea.

The cousins shared a glance between them, and Vale thought back to that time and how difficult it was for him. She was certain Caleb would never forget.

He slapped his hand on his thigh and his smile seemed genuine. "What's on our menu for supper?"

Vale swallowed a mouthful of cocoa. "Spaghetti and meatballs, garlic French bread, and a feta cheese salad." With brows arched, her eyes focused on Cherry. What would she say to that menu?

Caleb laughed. "Just so you know, Cherry, our French loaf isn't any old bread."

"It isn't?"

He waved a hand. "Oh, no, it's whole wheat French bread."

"Hmmm." Cherry now flipped through an ancient magazine she'd snatched off of the coffee table. "I enjoy the combination of whole wheat, butter, and garlic."

"Nice." Vale crossed her legs where she sat on the floor. "I'm a wholegrain nut. Have to have it daily."

Cherry angled her head. "Once again, Vale, I wanted to say I appreciate you allowing me to come."

Vale broke eye contact with Cherry and stared at her cocoa with three tiny marshmallows left floating. "We're glad you could." Did she mean this? The Lord knew she tried. It wasn't like Cherry made it hard. It was the whole jealous thing. At the clench of her jaw, she vowed to control her stubborn emotions.

Caleb added another two-foot-long madrone log onto the fire coals and brushed his palms together. "Anyone want to play Scrabble?"

"Sure," the women said. Vale grinned. This was one of the relaxing indoor activities she looked forward to on their annual trip.

They settled on the floor around the coffee table and laid the alphabet tiles upside down. Caleb's hand trembled, and Vale kept quiet until Cherry excused herself and left the room.

She leaned close enough to touch his sleeve. "What's wrong?"

He folded his hands together and hid them underneath the table. "It happens, though I don't know why. It's like they get the shakes, and I can't stop them."

Oh, no. Her stomach quivered and her nerves spiked.

Cherry's footsteps drew near, and she couldn't voice her concern in front of their company. He would be upset if she did. He stood and mumbled he needed to get the snacks. She gave herself a mental shake and picked three racks and placed them at each of their places. "So, Cherry, are you good at this game?" Her voice sounded as shaky as her insides. Could a person melt like Jell-O does in the sun? She added seven tiles to her holder. What was taking him so long?

"I win some."

She swallowed a chuckle. "I'm a loser but still enjoy it." She pointed across the table at Caleb's empty spot. "That guy wins most of our games." Any second she'd check on him. Would that be too motherly? She sighed. Changing a person's ways was no easy jaunt across a meadow.

As she moved her tiles around on the holder, a smoky scent made her nose twitch. She leaped from the sofa and ran toward the kitchen. Curled on the floor near the cook-stove, Caleb moaned and rocked, his breaths seemed ragged.

Her knees hit the floor next to him. "Cherry! Quick!" Cherry's shoes thumped at a run. She screeched to a halt in the doorway and gasped. Vale stabbed a finger toward the stove. "Shut the firebox door."

Vale hooked her arms under his shoulders and dragged him to the middle of the kitchen away from the stove. "And get the afghan off the sofa."

Behind her, the cast iron stove door clanked shut. In a sprint, Cherry dashed from the room and returned a moment later the blanket in her hands. Meanwhile, Vale settled his upper body on her lap. "Caleb, your face is solid sweat." His teeth chattered as if to disagree, and Cherry draped the afghan over him.

Tears streaked down the sides of his face as he gasped. "Can't. Breathe."

She pointed at the kitchen counter. "Get a wet cloth."

Vale glanced over her shoulder at Cherry as she stood, reached for the dishcloth drawer, and turned the faucet knob. Water gushed over a clean cloth. She knelt on one knee next to Vale and placed the damp cloth on his forehead. His lids fluttered, and he stiffened in Vale's arms. "Open the window above the sink."

Cherry rose. The window squeaked open as a breeze circulated. Vale studied his face. Soon, his body relaxed and his breaths became even.

As Cherry settled on the floor next to her, their shoulders touched. The simple contact blurred her vision. She blinked and willed herself not to cry. But when Cherry's hand smoothed back Caleb's hair ... tears drip, dripped and hit his shoulder. She gnawed on her bottom lip. What should she do? "Caleb? We're taking you to the emergency room."

He shook his head no.

She double blinked and let the last of her tears fall. Hadn't she given her word not to mother him? But. "I'm scared. And I don't understand these attacks."

Cherry agreed. "Me too."

His lips curved at the corners. "I'm okay."

Cherry wrung her hands on her lap, and her eyes so moist the tears would fall any second.

Vale smoothed her hand over the stubble on his cheek and waited for what seemed like forever for him to recover.

He lifted up onto his elbows, scooted backward, and rested against the cupboard. She smiled her encouragement as he rubbed both temples and nodded. "Good to go."

Vale stood to help Caleb as he pushed himself to his feet. He wobbled, and she gripped his arms. "Whoa."

His eyelids drooped. "I'm sorry I scared you."

Cherry cleared her throat. "Listen, I'm not comfortable with any of this. You need to go to the hospital."

Vale moved closer to her. "I agree."

"No, no. Really." He raked his fingers through the crown of his wavy brown hair. "I think this is because of the new medication."

Her every nerve jerked. "*Whhhaaat?*"

"Dang it." He fisted his hand on the counter. "The new meds took the edge off my migraines."

She gasped.

Cherry sniffled. "What exactly did Dr. Roger say about it?"

"He said it's used for depression but could help me keep my migraines away."

Vale bit her tongue to keep her anger squelched, even though her heartbeats raced. She snatched her phone off the table. "At least call the hospital."

Cherry raised her palms. "Can we get cell service?"

"We have before."

"Alright." He stared at her. "Find the hospital number, and I'll talk to them."

She did and handed him the phone. As he explained what he'd experienced to the person he spoke to, the girls stood nearby. At one point Caleb listened for long moments and then answered, "Oh, yeah, it has happened before but this was the worst. I think it's my new medication because my symptoms are some of the side effects that can happen." He listened again and nodded. "Yes, my pulse and my breathing are calm again. The dizzy spell is all but gone. What?" A long pause. "Okay."

He disconnected the call with a tap of his finger, and Vale leaped toward him. "Well?"

"The nurse agrees it's possible it could be the medication." He clapped his hands. "I'm starved." Both girls jumped. Caleb filled a water glass and he downed it in a few swallows. "I'll go back for a doctor appointment after our hunting trip."

She stiffened as though ice clogged her spine.

Cherry's shoulders slumped, and she left the kitchen.

He stared at Vale and his brow rose. "What?"

"I think she's upset about you waiting to see your doctor."

"That could be sooner if we both fill our tags right away."

"I'm mad at you." Vale poked him in the chest. "Why didn't you at least tell me you started a new med?" She slapped her leg. "You aren't alone here, but you seem to think so." Tears pierced her eyes.

He had the decency to bow his head.

She flapped a hand toward the entryway. "You better go check on her."

He did so, and his footsteps halted in the living room. Cherry and he spoke in low voices. Vale shuddered. It was too much to watch him act helpless twice in one week. She moved to the counter to begin their evening meal. She put tomato paste in a pot and tried hard not to listen to their conversation.

But she failed.

"Well, I should know a little, Caleb. It's my job environment."

He murmured.

"Fine, then, but don't blame the doctor when your symptoms ruin your life." Silence for several ticks of the clock. "Or worse."

He chuckled. "If it's worse, I won't be around to blame the doctor."

"This is *not* funny." She raised her voice. "I had a sister once."

Now Vale . . . peeked around the corner of the kitchen entryway. He took Cherry by the arm, opened the front door, and led her outside. Back in the kitchen and through the above-sink window, she stared at the pair where they stood underneath Papa's apple trees. Cherry's arms were crossed.

She turned her attention back to the spaghetti sauce and stirred it with the wooden spoon. What did Cherry mean about her sister?

At the bread board, she sliced the loaf of French bread lengthwise. She mixed butter, Himalayan salt, and garlic granules in a cup. She glanced out the window, but they were gone. On tiptoes, she leaned toward the window's right side and bent forward to scan the driveway. Caleb stood at Cherry's open car door. Her expression reminded Vale of a sad girl who'd had her heart shattered.

Cherry looked away from him and blinked.

Was she crying?

Maybe she lost a sister to a medical problem. Vale nodded. That would put her over the edge with Caleb's situation.

He spun on his heels and hurried toward the cabin. Vale met him at the door and opened her mouth to speak. His hand rose in the air before he passed.

Okay. But she followed him into the bedroom where the girls were to bunk for the night.

He stooped and grabbed Cherry's suitcase and her purse. He glared. "Seriously, Vale, this is not the time."

She moved from the bedroom doorway to let him by, and he walked out the open front door. Vale huffed, "Well," and settled at the kitchen window again.

He placed Cherry's things in her car, took a backward step, and shut the passenger door. She stepped on the gas pedal a little too hard and left him where he stood, hands stuffed in his jeans front pockets.

She wasn't sure how she felt that Cherry decided to leave. On one hand, she was sad. On the other, relieved, although she liked her.

Vale added more wood to the cook-stove, then added the meatballs to the cast iron skillet. A soft sizzle began underneath the meat. Kippy came in from who knew where. "I wonder, Kippy, if Caleb will still want to eat." Kippy whined, and did what she always did when she wanted a scratchin'. She rolled onto her back.

The front door opened and closed. Caleb's boot scuffed on the kitchen floor and stopped behind her. Still at the stove, she didn't move, didn't glance his way, but said the only thing that came to her. "We have too much food. Maybe Kippy would eat a plate of spaghetti and meatballs."

She faced him.

"Is this my fault too?" His expression had softened from earlier.

"Oh, Caleb." Vale grabbed him and squeezed. "I'm sorry about Cherry."

"At first, Cherry's reaction felt like a control thing."

She set the table as they talked. "What happened to her sister?"

He poured orange juice into a glass and took a long drink.

"She didn't say?"

"She died of an overdose of pills." He wiped his mouth. "She didn't say what kind, but it will be two years ago this December." His eyes misted. "She cried as she got into the car."

I saw. Vale sighed. "I'm sad for her. That would be like me losing you." She switched the toaster oven to bake and slid in the two halves of the garlic bread. "Hungry?"

Caleb guzzled the last of the juice. "I can eat."

She smiled and set out Nana's Depression-era green plates. "Good, me too. I could eat a horse." She slapped her mouth. "I can't believe I just said—"

"Nerves." Caleb set their forks on top of the napkins. "We've had a rough time."

"Yeah, this evening hasn't helped." They both finished setting the table and waited for the bread to toast. "I hope she can find her way out of here and to the freeway."

"She's a big girl. I did make her promise to call when she gets to the freeway entrance."

Vale sniffed. "Oh, no." She opened the door of the toaster oven and smoke billowed.

He grabbed the potholders and reached for the pan. "Here let me." He set the blackened bread on the stove top. "Burned but not wasted."

They each took a side of bread and scraped the charcoaled tops into the sink. "I always did hate this messy job." Vale nudged him with her elbow. "How about you?"

"Naw." He grinned at her. "I kinda' like the taste of burnt."

Settled at the table, Caleb said the blessing. "Thank you, Lord, for this food and for the one who prepared it. In Jesus' holy name. Amen."

She whisked her napkin to her lap. He dug in and served a large portion onto his plate. Vale gawked. "Seriously?"

His brows rose. "What?"

She pointed. "All that."

He scooped a forkful of spaghetti and twisted it around and shoved the mouthful past his lips.

Vale *tsk*ed and glanced at Caleb as he ate. Now, he re-heaped his plate. So unlike him, and wasn't it good to have a healthy appetite?

But. Could this be one of the side effects from the new medication? How many were there?

A COYOTE HOWLED. Three more followed in an ear-splitting song. She placed a pillow over her head. Morning would come early enough. The front door opened and shut. She swung her stocking feet over the side of the bed and the springs squeaked. She flicked on the lamp, scratched her back near her hip with a thumb nail, and yawned. The clock showed three a.m.

She found Kippy in front of the fireplace, where she shivered at Caleb's feet. That dog had always feared the coyote howls.

Vale stared at him as he warmed his back at the fire. "Did you just come inside?"

He nodded. "Last I heard, their yelps sounded like they were going away from our place. I think they smelled me."

He plopped onto the sofa, and she joined him. "Did Cherry call?"

He yawned. "She made it short and to the point."

Vale nibbled on the tip of a nail. "You think you'll see her again?"

His eyes grew round as pebbles. "I sure hope so."

"What do you like about her?"

"She's kind, and I feel comfortable around her. Cute, too. And her naturally ginger hair?" He whistled.

"How do you know her hair is natural?"

"I can tell."

She tucked her feet underneath her. "To feel comfortable in a relationship is important. You know, I've not found someone like that." Vale squirmed at her confession. "I hope I will one day." An image surfaced of Dr. Peterson. His crinkly eyes when he smiled. His thick black waves— *Stop*. She blinked.

"Now, Vale." Caleb turned to the fire. "It'll happen. You wait and see."

She stretched her arms above her head. "And maybe right now, I don't need anyone." The doctor's image again. Had she lied? She huffed a breath.

He added another log to the heaped embers within the fireplace. "Are you saying I need Cherry?"

She shrugged. "Maybe so and maybe I'm not. Besides, what do I know about love?"

"Speak your mind, Vale." He straightened and wiped debris from his palms.

"Well, I look at it this way. It's important to feel comfortable. I figure, that lack in a relationship might mean we don't need that person."

He rubbed the heel of his palm over his eyes. "It's too late for deep thoughts."

"You mean early." She placed a hand on her hip. "Look at the time. Why weren't you sleeping? You don't feel well?"

"I was, but those coyotes woke me." He jutted his chin toward the fireplace. "I was on the floor near the fire. Me and Kip."

"Oh, good." She yawned again and stood. "If we lose too much sleep, we won't be able to get an early start on our first day of hunting. Night, Caleb."

He grabbed the afghan and curled within it on the floor. "See you, bright and later."

Vale snickered. "Yeah, you wish. I'm hauling you off that floor as planned." She left the living room and went to bed. She didn't think to ask Caleb why he preferred the floor next to the fire instead of the bed. Was he that cold?

Is being cold another symptom?

10~THOUGH I WALK
CALEB

LIKE SOMEONE WHO had turned on himself, Caleb became a midnight owl.

All his life, he hadn't been much good for anything after eight o'clock. He'd always walked around half asleep until going to bed. Not anymore. When Vale went to bed, he tried the floor in front of the fireplace. As a boy, it was his favorite spot to sleep when he spent the night in the cabin. Tonight, it didn't work, so he warmed milk in a pan on the cook-stove where a few coals were left. Cocoa would relax him. He searched the cupboards for the can. Every food item had its own container of glass or tin to keep the mice from eating their fill. Nana had set up the kitchen ages ago, and her family kept it that way. All except the teas they bought last year.

He located the cocoa and next to it a jar labeled *MARSHMELOS*, in Nana's print. He chuckled. Nana never claimed she could spell. The bridge of Caleb's nose smarted as tears gathered. The jar in his hand blurred. He missed her. Almost as much as he did his parents. He had to stop and count how many years ago he and Vale's grandparents had been gone. Nana four, Papa almost one. The hurt of it still smacked Caleb when he least expected.

He poured the tepid milk into a mug, and wandered into the living room. By the fireplace he sipped his cocoa. When the mug was still half full, his eyes grew heavy and he rubbed his scalp. He stared through the plate glass window into the dark. As a kid, he couldn't count how many times this window was the last thing he saw before he closed his eyes and slept.

Just as his eyelids winked to a half droop, a shadow crossed closer to the ground outside the window. He jolted upright. It could have been a ghost, though the only Ghost he believed in had Holy placed in front of the name. He went outside and a coyote yipped. Three more yapped in response. Not a big deal. So he walked back into the cabin to get some sleep.

He passed the living room and flopped on his bed. Cherry's misty eyes, her mouth turned down at the corners came into focus as his lashes closed. He had asked her, "Will I see you again?" She stared at him in silence and moments later, she pulled from his driveway and disappeared at the bend in the road.

He settled on his side and prayed, "Lord, if she's not for me . . .." He continued his prayers and ended in, "Jesus' name. Amen."

Bwhoom!

Jolted awake, Caleb blinked, rolled from bed, and tugged on his jeans. "What in the name of Moses?"

A high-pitched *whoopee*, and another *bwhoom!* He stumbled over his own feet and opened the front door. Twenty yards away near the side of the cabin, Vale held her arms out stiff while she held a pistol. "Vale." She didn't move. He cupped his hands around his mouth. "*Valie.*"

She twisted away from the paper target and dislodged the ear plugs. "Hey, Caleb. I sighted in my pistol."

"With two shots?" He rubbed his palms over his face.

"Boy, were you asleep or what?" She sauntered toward him, her grin as wide as the Rogue River. "That was my twelfth shot, Mr. Cutter." She pulled out a baggie from her pocket and shook the shells. "See?" She flung the bag through the air, and he caught it. "Count them."

He raked his free hand through his bed-head hair. "Good grief, Vale, you'll wake the whole forest."

She flailed her arms in severe dramatics. "It's daylight, for pity sake." She cocked her head. "Is *your* pistol sighted? Ya don't want to pull off a cock-eyed shot if a cougar leaps out at ya." She snickered.

"Yes, Miss Smarty Pants. I sighted it before our trip." He moved back toward the cabin, and said over his shoulder, "Coffee." He pulled open the screen door and dropped the baggie of shells on the entryway table. "Women."

Vale shouted. "I heard that, and you know coffee is bad."

In the kitchen, she peeked over his shoulder, while he grabbed the handle of the coffee pot and poured. "Yeah, yeah, Vale, it strips my B vitamins. I've got it memorized."

Her bottom lip puckered. "Don't mock me."

Anticipating his first swallow of the brew, his brows bounced. "If you're so against coffee, why did you make me some? Huh?"

"Well, you're used to drinking it in the mornings, besides you'd get a headache without it."

"I have enough of those, that's for sure." He slurped on his coffee, closed his eyes and said, "Aww."

She pointed at the clock on the kitchen wall. "We've missed our first morning hunt, you know."

Caleb yawned, and gulped more coffee. "I'm sorry, but I couldn't sleep. After breakfast, we'll ride the horses on the Mt. Baldy trail. See what we can see for an afternoon hunt." He shrugged. "Besides, we wouldn't have gone hunting today if Cherry had stayed."

"Right." She broke four eggs into a bowl. "We're going to our tree stand where we spotted the buck this last spring, right?"

"The one that had the four-by-five antlers?" His eyes grew wide. "He's a beaut."

She whipped the eggs with a wire whisk. "Ready for scrambled eggs and muffins?"

Eyes mere slits, he wagged his head. "Are the muffins whole grain?"

"Of course," Vale raised her chin, "we can't go hunting with processed food and white flour in our guts."

He waved her off as though swatting a pesky gnat. "You're a broken record."

She glanced at him. "You're healthier because of Ma and me. And you know it."

In between coffee swallows, he drank a glass of water, a required regiment since he became a part of Vale's family all those years ago. "Man, this place has the best tasting water." He stared at the eggs she whipped to liquefy. "Did you already eat?"

She set the skillet on the stove and added more wood to the fire box. "Oh, yeah. Hours ago, lazy bones."

"I'm here aren't I?" He pulled out a chair and sat. "I can't help it when I'm wide awake almost all night."

Vale dropped two halves of the muffins in the toaster and pressed the lever. "I know." She stirred the eggs on the stove into a fluff. "I'm impatient."

"You think?" He rose from his chair, extended his plate, and she dished his breakfast into his platter. "Just the way I like, not too done." He kissed her cheek.

"You're the best, Cuz." His muffins popped up in the toaster, and she set those on his plate.

As he ate, she rinsed the cast iron skillet in the sink, sprinkled baking soda on the inside, and gently scrubbed. "Well, thank you, you're the best too." Counters clean, she dried her hands. "I'll saddle the horses."

Caleb shoveled in a mouthful of egg, chewed, and swallowed. "Okay, be there in a few." When she left, a mental list of gear needed filtered through his mind. Gloves. Flashlight. A cap. Sunglasses. He finished off his eggs, grabbed the second muffin, and stuffed it in his shirt pocket. He munched on it as he retrieved their two small trail backpacks from a corner on the kitchen floor and set them on the table. Bags stuffed, they also included some wire rope, a water bottle, three energy bars each, and a poncho in case it rained. To his belt, he strapped on the sheath that held his skinning knife.

Kippy stayed close to Vale's heels as they both entered the kitchen. She pointed. "What about Kip?"

"She stays home." He squatted before her and hugged her neck. She barked and pranced in place. "Sorry, girl. No can go." He stood and retrieved his bow and arrows off the living room wall mount.

Vale lifted her pack from the table, grabbed her bow, and headed out the door. He locked the cabin, and her eyes glimmered in what could only be excitement. "Ready, Cuz?"

He tipped his camouflage cap and waved for her to lead the way.

Mounted on their horses, he followed her on the paved road and toward the trail they would take. She twisted in the saddle. "Isn't this the best?"

He nodded. Hunting excited Vale as it did him, and he wanted the meat. If this was the way to get fresh game, then he was a hunter. Of course a guy would be proud to bring down a four-by-five buck. This year that certain buck would have an even larger set of antlers. He clicked his tongue and urged Storming into a trot to keep in pace alongside Vale.

On a wider trail, they rode side by side. They climbed Mt. Baldy as a headache ticked, ticked at the front of his head. He stopped his horse. "I forgot to bring my medication."

Her jaw slacked. "Let's go back."

"You don't have to go." She reined Princess round in answer. Before they got halfway there, the leather reins dampened from his sweaty palm.

BY THE TIME the cabin came into view, his migraine roared, full blown. He retrieved his pistol at a rustle in the brush nearby. Closer to the cabin, he attempted to stash his pistol back into its leather holder at his waist. It slipped from his hand and fell to the ground. Vale dismounted. "Here, let me help."

He got off Storming, but his legs wobbled more like cooked noodles than muscle, tendons, and bone. Caleb gripped the saddle horn and leaned into his horse to stay upright. His vision blurred. She settled the pistol into its holder on his hip.

Her cheeks quivered. "Let's walk the horses."

"I don't think I can get back on right now, anyway."

"Would you rather I get the pill and bring it to you?""

He shook his head no as he concentrated on each step. *Walk, walk, walk.*

Although it felt like he'd crawled ten miles, Caleb stood in the kitchen. He popped a pill on his tongue and drank straight from the orange juice bottle. Kippy tapped danced on the worn linoleum, but he ignored the silly pup.

As he slumped on a chair, he waited for the crazy symptoms to disappear. Kippy rested her muzzle on one of his moccasined feet.

Vale nodded from where she leaned against the refrigerator. "Should I call the doctor?"

"Nah, I can wait."

She crossed her arms. "Don't mess around, Caleb."

Long minutes later the pain eased. "Hey, girl." Kippy jumped to attention as though she waited for a command. "Relax. You're an indoor dog for the week." She barked as he scratched her behind the ear.

"Feel better?" Vale's brow pinched.

"Yep."

Thirty minutes later, the pain had receded to a dull ache, and then disappeared completely. He grabbed a root beer pop for the road and locked the door behind them.

THEY HAD RIDDEN side by side for a short distance on the dirt road, when Vale cleared her throat. "I'm trying hard not to mother you."

He leaned forward in the saddle, wrists crossed over the saddle horn. "I appreciate that."

"Did I pass the test?"

He tipped his cap high on his forehead. "Yep."

Her eyes glistened. "You're sure?"

"You're doing better."

Her toe nudged his leg. "We're almost adults."

"I forgot." Caleb furrowed his brows. "In two days we turn twenty."

"No longer teens." She subjected him to a razor-sharp inspection through narrowed eyes. "You're no quitter."

"True." Although, he was tired. If only he knew how long before he would be his old self once again. But, only God had that answer.

They continued their ride through well-used deer trails to higher elevations. He halted Storming. The trees on both sides opened to a mountain view which stole his breath. Every. Single. Time. He grinned as the tension eased from his gut through his chest and gushed from his shoulders like a gust of wind. Miles and miles of small and large mountains studded with trees of fir, pine, maple, and his favorite—the red madrone. He not only enjoyed the beauty like no other tree, but it made the best hardwood for stove fires.

Vale's sigh came soft as a whisper. "I love this country. I plan to never leave. Before I marry," she twisted in the saddle to face him, "my future husband has to agree we'll stay here forever." She waved her arm to include the view. "I'll even make him sign an agreement to my wishes."

He grinned. "You'll fall in love and never remember what you said."

"Nuh-uh." She wagged her head, and her single braid flapped from arm to arm.

"Yeah-uh." He shook a finger at her. "You're a pushover for people you love, Sunny Vale."

"We're wasting time." Her brows squished together. "I've got an appointment with a buck." She clicked her tongue at Princess and walked her on the elevated trail along Mt. Baldy's ridge.

Caleb glanced at his watch. Four hours before legal hunting time ended. They entered an area he judged was a five-year growth of planted fir trees on the west side.

Vale pulled back on the reins and stopped, while he and Storming came along side. "We ready to sit in our tree stand?"

She mouthed, "Yep."

They dismounted and led the horses to a grassy flat area. They attached lead ropes to allow the horses to graze. The horses got right to the business of ripping up weeds, and the cousins pulled their small backpacks from the saddles.

He hoisted his pack on his shoulders, licked his finger, and stuck it in the air to check the wind direction. A soft breeze cooled his finger. He gave the thumbs up. The deer wouldn't smell them, unless the wind changed to hit their backs.

Vale nodded at him as she tugged her brown knitted hat over her forehead. She pulled on her pack and readjusted the straps. Her bow in hand, she sauntered toward their trail.

Caleb bent on one knee to retie a moccasin lace, and the ground whirled.

11~VALLEY OF THE SHADOW
VALE

AN ORCHESTRA OF songbirds echoed in the forest and the horses munched, munched as the bits in their mouths jingled. She raised her chin to the sky and opened her arms. Oh, how she missed the familiar greenery of mountains when she wasn't smack dab in the middle.

A rustling *thump*. She glanced over a shoulder.

Caleb.

Sprawled on the ground.

Her nerves zinged.

As she sprinted, her gear flapped against her back. When she reached him, he stayed still as death. Her heart cantered within her chest, and she knelt next to him, and touched his cheek. "Caleb? Can you hear me?" She shrugged off her pack.

His lashes fluttered, and her heart skipped and dipped. She leaned closer and grabbed his wrist and sighed in relief at his strong pulse. She pulled the canteen from her belt and poured water onto a hanky and wrung out the excess moisture. She placed the cool cloth on his forehead. He moaned. Her limbs began to tremble. She whispered, "We are all alone." What would she do if he needed more help this time than she could give him?

How would she get him in the saddle so she could lead him down the mountain?

But not alone. Vale stilled and blinked. Did those words come from her mind? It seemed so. But then it was different. Soothing. She bowed her head. "Dear Father, please. Help."

"Praying for me?"

She jumped at his voice and laid her cheek on his shoulder. Her muffled sobs filled the quiet forest. "Oh, Caleb."

"None of that." He sat upright, and the hanky fell to his lap. She settled more comfortably on the ground next to him as he said, "I don't know what happened." His hands went to each side of his head. "Hurts."

She sniffled and wiped her nose on a sleeve. "I thought the pills were working for the pain at least."

He pulled his legs toward his chest. "Me too."

"Here." She moved the canteen to his mouth.

He gulped and swallowed and drank some more, while she studied his features. Something seemed different about him. His round face as a boy had been long gone as he matured. But that wasn't it. She clenched her jaw. "Did you know you have dark shadows under your eyes?"

Caleb touched below his lower lashes.

"It makes you look pale." She pursed her lips. "I'm taking you to the doctor. Now. You need to tell him—"

"Stop." He held his palm out as though to defend himself from her words. "Quit."

Her mouth opened. She closed it shut. Her fear for him simmered now in anger. "You're so stubborn." She jerked away and stood.

"I know all the weird stuff affecting me." His eyes narrowed. "But you women are too pushy." He spit the last words.

She snatched the hanky off the ground as her anger sparked like a lightning strike. "*Excuse* me! I thought you said I was doing good. Besides, this could be a matter of life or death."

After she grabbed her gear, she walked the twenty yards toward their trail. So be it. She was done. The mule-headed, male-ego . . .. But. Vale had to look back and check on him. He brushed himself off, pulled his pack on, and grabbed his bow off the ground. He glared at her.

She gave him the stink eye right back. *Men.*

Caleb checked his watch, so she checked hers. She would ignore him, this, this person who had changed before her eyes. Since when did he complain about women? Right. Never.

She inhaled and eased her breath on the exhale. Vale had to get a grip. One thing she knew for sure, though. If he had another attack, she'd drag him to his horse one way or another and take him to the emergency room. She'd show his stubborn behind. And no coddling either.

She puckered her mouth in determination. What did Nana always say? "There's always a plan B."

Vale decided to let him catch up. Just because she could spit tacks about now didn't mean she no longer cared. When he reached her, they walked on at the same pace. She watched for the madrone tree, their clue for where they would take the narrower trail about sixty yards farther. When the tree came into view, she pointed. He nodded.

They approached the entrance to the trail as it branched on the right. They would be silent now. Not that she wanted to discuss anything further. To her way of thinking, his life was more important than hunting. A snort rose in her throat, but she swallowed. She used to think hunting was the most important thing. But not this year. Not so long as Caleb had the strange attacks.

The two cousins made their way along the narrow path, quiet as snakes through the leaves. Every few steps they stopped, looked, and listened. The underbrush grew thick and allowed for only a few bare spots large enough for a deer to bed down, unseen from a distance. She hoped to glimpse an antler. Or maybe a muzzle stretched along the ground as a buck napped. Black-tail deer. She shook her head. They were the smartest deer on earth. They were much harder to hunt than any other species of deer, and with the brush like this to hide under. To bring in a buck every year? Only the very best hunters could do that, and Papa had done so.

A tickle grew in her throat, and she pressed her nose against her arm. Scotch broom. She was so allergic to it and there it was, a few yellow flowers left on the branches. She tiptoed past the nasty stuff. If she coughed, she would give them away to any deer in the vicinity. Soon, Caleb's soft footsteps signaled he was closer behind. He poked her back. His signal to hurry. She bristled, but then she thought of the hunt and let it go.

Beneath the stand, she placed her moccasin on the first steel bar of the ladder. Once she reached the top of the metal mesh floor, she stood in the right corner. Caleb followed. He settled on the left and released a soft breath.

A Steller's jay scolded from one of the trees, tattle telling to nearby creatures. She kneeled and grumped in a low whisper, "Ding-dong bird."

He tapped a finger to his lips and lifted his binoculars where they were attached by a leather strap around his neck. She did the same and scoped from right to the middle of her view. He scoped from left to the middle of his view. Mainly, though, they watched below them at a space of clearing that ended their sixty-yard-long trail. This path, though, continued past the tree stand and led down to the base of Mt. Baldy. As Papa had trained them, Vale kept her ears alert to the rustle of leaves. The snap of twigs on the ground.

What seemed to be the same Steller's jay flapped its wings and squawked, once again, and then the forest grew so quiet you could hear an acorn drop. She stuck her pointer finger in her mouth and clamped to moisten. Then, she slipped it out and lifted her finger high in the air. Not even a breeze. The deer couldn't smell them. Not yet anyway. If the wind changed and they caught human scent, the cousins would be busted. The hunt for this location would be over.

On their left, leaves on the ground rustled. Twigs snapped. Silence. She gripped Caleb's arm and squeezed. He lifted his binoculars and scanned the area. Whatever stirred the earth headed their way. It snorted and blew its breath. As sure as the sun brightened the day, it was a buck. Vale cocked her head and calculated it at a distance of thirty yards.

The rustling began again, like a Spanish dance. This buck would tear clods from the ground. The cousins inserted their broad head arrows in place. Because Caleb stood the closest to the buck, she would back him if needed. Probably not. He excelled as a sharpshooter.

Closer and closer the buck danced their way. He snorted again. Grunted. Another rush of wind released through his nose raised goose bumps along Vale's arms. Antlers, at least a four point, flashed within the brush's slice of spaces. Her heart banged. Caleb pulled back the string.

She raised her bow, set her right-handed release into the small hole on the string, and extended her elbow straight to the side. Ready to pull back, she waited for him to take his best shot.

The buck jerked his regal head—majestic antlers, more proof he stood like a king of the forest. The noises he made pumped Vale's heart so fast, she panted. His front shoulder came into view for the perfect shot. She pulled the string.

At a sudden shift of Caleb's weight, his arm touched her bow near her relaxed hand which cradled the bow. His arrow shot—a pitiful plop too close to them on the ground—the buck bolted. Caleb's body slumped. She released the string. *No, no, no.*

The color of his face had paled and sweat dotted his forehead.

Vale leaned her bow against the stand, the broad head arrow still notched in place and faced toward the forest. "Caleb!"

SHE CONCENTRATED ON not flipping out. She wet the hanky from the canteen and spread the cool material across his forehead once again. He groaned. She whispered, "It's okay, Cuz. I'm here."

His eyes fluttered. "Wh—?"

"Shhh. Rest." She lifted the bandana higher on his forehead and away from his eyes. "We're in no hurry to move." Was that a lie? She prayed he could get his balance enough to make the climb down.

He wagged his head where he lay on the hard metal mesh surface and touched his temple. "I blacked out again?"

She squatted on her heels. "I'm taking you to the hospital."

He placed a palm on the bottom of the tree stand and moved as though to rise. She pushed on his shoulder. "Relax."

"No." He winced. "The buck."

"He's gone." She uncapped the canteen and motioned for him to drink. As he sipped the water, she let go of a long sigh. She had to watch what she said about exiting the forest. "Did you notice he has six points to each side of his antlers?"

He blinked and gazed over her shoulder. "I'm sorry. I fouled. Big time." He muttered. "Dad-gummit. What a miserable day." His eyelids drooped.

Vale sat and dangled her legs over the side. "I don't think our buck saw or smelled us, so there's always tomorrow." She cleared her throat. "If you're feeling better." What was she saying? He needed rest. In a hospital bed. Nurses to care for him. She lowered her voice so as not to sound bossy. "What worries me most, Caleb, is you." She licked her mouth. "I think your medicine is dangerous." Oops. There she went again. Would he challenge her?

"I'd be a fool not to notice."

Her limbs relaxed.

He removed the damp hanky and gave it back to her. "I'd say you may be right."

She raised a hand. "And you need to go to the emergency room. Now."

He shook his head no. "I'll be fine." He looked around. "My bow."

Vale groaned. No. More like a growl at his thick-headed ideas. *He's going to give me gray hairs already.* She pointed to the ground. "It fell when you slumped over." What she really wanted was to shake some sense into his brain, but that would only give him a worse headache. She blew air between her lips. It would be a long rest of the day to get him to the hospital.

He frowned at her. "I'll need to shoot a couple of arrows to make sure the sights are still perfect. For the bow to fall a second time and from this height, it's out of focus." He brushed a hand over his face as though irritated. "We brought a target bag, right?"

"There's always one here in the barn." She tipped her chin to the side, determined to play along.

"Let's go back to the cabin." He stood. "I need to test my sites."

Good. They'd be going in the right direction for a hospital trip.

Caleb led the way down from the stand, and retrieved his bow, and wiped the dirt off. Her heart ticked an exited thump at how easy this could play out. She imagined the drive to Griffins Pass. When she jumped off the last rung, a movement in the brush snagged her attention. Caleb stilled. Out of habit, she again locked her arrow in the bowstring and waited. Cinnamon fur scurried and disappeared.

He whispered, "It's small."

She lowered her bow. "Time to scoot out of here."

Both took a few forward steps. The critter bleated. A louder and longer bleat responded.

Vale glanced at Caleb. "It's a fawn and its mother."

"Let's go."

As they moved, the doe sprinted, and the fawn followed in a leap.

She chuckled. "So doggone cute." She stepped on a log along the path and walked it.

"Yep." Caleb caught her arm as she stumbled across the log. "Be careful."

She *tsk*ed. Who's supposed to help who?

The horses still grazed where they had left them. With equipment packed, the cousins mounted and retraced their way back to the cabin. Vale rubbed her neck to ease a kink. Exhausted beyond belief, she figured it was because she worried so much about Caleb.

As she made the corner in sight of the cabin, she halted Princess with a tug on the reins. "Is that Cherry's car?" The shiny red Volkswagen appeared out of place in the rustic setting. Like it had before. Vale stuffed back a groan. She really did like Cherry, but it seemed she came into their lives at a rotten time.

He halted Storming alongside Princess. "Mercy me."

Cherry brushed herself off from where she had been sitting on the porch steps. Vale lowered her voice. "Your girlfriend is back."

He shot her a look. "Be nice." He waved. "Hey, Cherry."

She grinned, one meant only for him. At least that's what it looked like.

Vale grumbled under her breath but grew ashamed. Hadn't she come to terms with this already? A girl in his life? As she walked toward the barn to unsaddle, brush, and feed Princess a slice of hay, Caleb matched her steps. He handed over Storming's reins. "Would you?" His eyes pleaded.

"Sure." She figured his visit would be short. They had a hospital trip to take.

12~FEAR NO EVIL
CALEB

HIS ANGER OF two hours ago at "the women" scattered like rocks beneath a mountain goat's climb.

Caleb's chin slacked at the sight of Cherry's car in front of the cabin. Confused, he kneaded the back of his neck with his knuckles. Is this a good sign? He prayed it was so. From the moment he laid eyes on her at the doctor's office, he couldn't erase her from his mind. With each step closer to her, his heart whirled like a chain saw.

She grinned.

When he reached her they embraced.

His jaw caressed her hair, and he inhaled the fruity scent of tangerine. He loved tangerines.

"I'm sorry." She spoke near his ear. "I acted like a brat."

He stepped away, and his hands slid down her bare arms. "You were scared."

She licked her lips. "May I stay?"

His heart muscles kicked like a colt. "Sure, sure. Let's tell Vale." He wrapped an arm over her shoulders and guided her to the barn. "We have an overnight guest."

Vale hovered above one of the grain pans where each horse ate their meal. She dumped a slice of hay in each stall. Did she just clench her jaw? He tapped her shoulder. "Vale?"

She straightened. "I heard." Her face void of emotion, she faced Cherry. "If he has another attack, I need you to stay calm. Can you do that?"

Cherry's lashes fluttered as though she hadn't expected the question. She puckered her lips, long moments passed, and she raised her chin. "I can, and I will."

She drew closer and placed hands on her hips. "You're welcome here, if you don't ditch Caleb, again. That's the deal." She pointed. "And another thing. That doctor of yours is a quack."

Cherry took a backward step, and Caleb's arm dropped from her shoulder.

"Vale." He drew out her name in warning.

"No, no." Cherry nodded. "I respect her honesty, and I agree about the new medication." She drew a deep breath. "That's actually why I came back. I have bad news and good news."

Vale put out a hand. "Listen. Before you say anymore, I'm taking Caleb to the hospital. Right now."

He hooked his thumbs on his belt buckle. "Oh, no, you're not."

"Yes. We are."

Cherry glanced from one to the other cousin. "Did something happen?"

Vale explained about the tree stand incident. When she finished, he spread his hands. "I'm not going, Vale. Besides, let's hear what Cherry has to say."

"Listen, the both of you," Cherry lifted her palm, "the bad news first. I did research on the medication prescribed to you. I believe you're suffering from some of the side effects."

Vale smoothed fingers through wayward strands of hair. "We already knew this."

"What you may not be aware of is two things." Cherry held a finger in the air. "First, you can't just quit these pills cold turkey—"

"What?" Vale gasped. "No way."

Caleb shuffled his moccasin feet as he glanced at Vale.

Her eyes became mere slits. "You knew this?"

He looked away.

Cherry continued. "Because if you quit cold turkey it will bring on worse migraines. And." Her second finger rose in the air. "The other thing is this medication was not originally prescribed for headaches."

Vale's jaw lowered. "For what then?"

"For depression and anxiety."

Vale shot him another glare. "You knew that too, didn't you?"

He nodded.

"I can't imagine what you've been through, Caleb, but there's got to be a better way." Cherry touched his arm and blinked at him as if pleading. "This drug is a gamble that doesn't always work for your problem."

Vale snorted. "You think?"

He crossed his arms and grunted.

Cherry's fingers slid off his arm. "I'll go back to work and get you a squeezed-in appointment for the Monday after your vacation. Because the good news is you could try a natural remedy to help get some relief for your migraines before the meds are completely out of your system. There are also acupuncture clinics for migraines."

Caleb recalled what Dr. Peterson said about acupuncture.

"Wait, wait, wait." Vale sliced her hand through the air. "I still say he needs to go to the hospital. Today."

The two cousins shared a glance, and Caleb read sincere concern in Vale's wider than normal eyes.

Cherry touched his arm. "I can get you information on acupuncture if you decide to try it. Now I have something you can do right now." She reached in a knitted purse and produced two tiny bottles. "These are essential oils. One is lavender and the other is ginger."

"Wow." Caleb cocked a brow. "You're suggesting these might lessen my migraines?"

Her cheeks grew rosy. "Not might—it will give you relief, especially the lavender oil. I'm just not sure how much relief."

Vale squinted. "My mom uses essential oils."

Cherry tapped a nail on the bottle of lavender oil. "He should massage this one into his temples at the onset of pain, or it won't work as well." She pointed to the ginger. "This one will increase circulation to the brain and is used in a hot-as-you-can-stand foot bath."

He chuckled. "I'll try anything at this point."

"Good." Cherry handed him the bottles.

He examined each one. "When do I start?"

She clapped her hands. "Immediately?"

Vale stared at the bottle. "I'm all for natural. Something made by God." She narrowed her eyes at him. "But. You're still going to the emergency."

Cherry leaned in. "If Vale thinks you should then so do I."

"No, I won't, we're on vacation. So you two can stop being nags." He unscrewed the cap on the lavender and sniffed. "Smells good and strong."

Caleb did not miss the glance Cherry and Vale gave each other. But he would not be coerced.

CALEB SCRAPED HIS chair along the worn linoleum as he pushed back with his feet. He cracked his knuckles. "Good meal, ladies." They had given him mostly the silent treatment after their disagreement over an ER visit. He'd try again to get them to say more than one-word sentences.

"Thanks." Cherry nodded.

He cleared off the table. "Why don't we have a Bible study?"

The beverage glass Cherry wiped dry stilled in her hand.

Vale washed a plate as she gazed at her. "Do you attend services, Cherry?"

"Well, I used to, but I quit two years ago." She set the glass in the cupboard. "I'm not sure where I stand spiritually."

"Hmm." Vale dove into washing another dish.

"What Vale means," Caleb shook crumbs from a dish cloth over the trash basket, "we've been attending the same church all our lives. We learned about God, His Son Jesus. That Jesus died for our sins, and we were baptized."

Cherry studied the floor. She moved a step to rinse the dishes that Vale washed. Caleb finished wiping off the table as the food in his gut settled like rocks. *Did we offend her?*

"I'm not happy where my parents are attending, so—"

Vale grabbed the plates and the platter. In his opinion, she scrubbed harder than necessary for chicken salad smears. "Sometimes people don't agree, right Cuz?"

"That's for sure."

Is she going to bring up the hospital thing again? She'd been frosty toward him the whole evening.

"You know." Cherry rinsed a plate. "I've worshiped in a church setting all my life. I don't feel any closer to God since I was a child."

He halted the broom in mid-sweep.

Vale's scour pad stilled on a pan. "Huh."

As he leaned an arm on the broom, he prayed he would say the words so as not to offend them. "I know several people our age who feel this way, and they've stopped their worship practices."

Vale kept her eyes on her work. "Why do you think?"

"Well." He rubbed a finger across his upper lip. "I have my ideas." Here was where she would split a temple vein. "I've talked to them, and I agree."

She jerked her head his way. "Seriously?"

He shrugged.

She scrubbed a pan like a bear scratches his back on a tree. "And here I thought you were skipping church because of your *pain.*"

Cherry's brows rose as she continued to dry dishes. "I'd really like to understand so maybe I can sort through my confusion."

"Honestly, I—" A high-pitched scream from outside cutoff Caleb's words. Cherry bolted to Vale's side. Kippy ran under the kitchen table and screeched like a scared kitten.

He chuckled.

"It's a cougar." She shrugged off Cherry's grip on her arm.

Cherry hugged her ribs and giggled. "Oh, sure." She squared her shoulders. "I've heard them before. Just last year, actually." She glanced through the kitchen window above the sink. "It wasn't as loud as this one, though." She visibly trembled.

The cousins shared a glance. His chuckle grew to a rumble in his throat. He swallowed down the laughter, though, so as not to make fun of Cherry's reaction. But Vale's shoulders shook and her eyes gleamed.

Cherry faced them and gasped. "Wh, what?" She moved to the counter and put a dried plate on the cupboard shelf. "You're both making fun of me."

He forced all expression from his face.

"Just say it." She clicked her tongue. "I'm the city girl who doesn't fit into your world, or your idea of church attendance, either." When she raised her chin at Vale, tears dotted her lashes.

"Now, Cherry." He stepped closer.

Vale bent forward as she held her stomach, her laughter escalated to raucous guffaws. She waved her hand around. "I—I—I'm—"

Cherry took a backward step. Her eyes grew round in her heart-shaped face. "She's crying?"

"She's not." He talked above Vale's now uncontrollable giggle hic-ups. "She does this. Ever since I can remember."

"We need to help her." Her finger pointed at Vale. "She's going to hyperventilate any second." She opened drawers in the kitchen. "Where's a paper sack?"

"No, she'll be fine." He draped an arm over Cherry's shoulder. "Though, she'll run to the bathroom any second."

"Why?"

"Umm." He tapped his chin with a finger and stared at the ceiling. "How do I say this nicely?"

"Oh." A blush rose on Cherry's cheeks as Vale's eyes streamed in laughter tears. "She needs to use the restroom because of laughing too hard."

At that moment, Vale pivoted and stumbled from the kitchen.

"See?" One corner of his mouth lifted. "What'd I tell you?"

Cherry's lips parted.

While Vale hic-upped in the bathroom, the cougar screamed again and drowned all sounds she made.

This time, Cherry jumped straight into his arms, but stiffened. "I'm not really scared of the cougar anymore." She pulled away, her arms at her sides. "I startle at sudden, loud noises."

He couldn't resist his protective emotions toward her, and he caressed her cheek. "It's okay, Ginger."

She soft punched his shoulder as her nose wrinkled. "What'd you call me that?"

"Ow." He rubbed the spot. "Because of the color of your hair." He sensed they were back on good terms again. His heart beat double time.

"I'll allow it." She chuckled. "I'm having fun here."

"Me, too. We were only teasing you about the cougar. It's smart to fear them."

She angled her head. "Yes, but I want to prove I'm not a scaredy-cat."

Vale poked her flushed face into the kitchen entryway. "I'm really not that mean. Right, Cuz?"

"Right." He meant to say more but a stab of pain pierced his head, and he closed his eyes and moaned.

"Caleb?" A swoosh of warmth and the women grabbed his elbows.

"Ahhh." He muttered. "Make it stop."

They led him to the sofa. "Sit, Caleb. Cherry, bring the pillow off his bed."

Soon they had him stretched out, but still the room spun like a windstorm among the trees. He shut his eyes and told himself to breathe. *God, please, it hurts.*

Vale mumbled something about cold turkey.

"No." Cherry's breath caressed his face. "You know he has to wean himself off this med. I'll be right back." She left the room and soon returned. "I'm going to apply the lavender tincture, Caleb, but point to where it hurts most." He touched his temples, and she massaged in the oil. He relaxed when the nice scent filled his nostrils and eased that area on his skin. She stopped and applied more on the other side.

Even though he lost track of time, at some point he sighed in relief. "Feels wonderful."

Cherry continued to massage. "Vale, would you heat water but don't let it get too hot? And the rinse water pan is the perfect size to soak his feet."

"Okay."

"I'll add drops of ginger into the water, and we'll have him sit and put his bare feet into the pan."

"Sure." Vale rose from where she sat at Caleb's feet. As she worked in the kitchen, he became aware of everything she did. He knew Nana's kitchen well. She added more wood to the cook-stove and the snap, crackle told him it flamed. Cherry's soft fingertips relaxed him further, and before he knew it, he fell asleep . . .. "Caleb? You need to sit now."

The massage was over. He cracked a grin. "Yes, boss." He opened one eye, and Vale's face hovered over him.

He sat upright before the women unlaced his moccasins, pulled them and his socks off, and rolled his pant legs to his calves. Cherry directed him. "Test the water to make sure it's not too hot."

He stuck a big toe in and dunked both feet into the pan. "Perfect." He rested the back of his head against the sofa. Would this ginger water really work?

Cherry touched his arm. "You act as if you have less pain?"

"Yes. Thank you." The room grew quiet, except for a popping sound. He opened one eye. Vale pulled her knuckles. A sure sign she was beyond stressed.

"It's okay, Valie."

THE SHADOW OF night filled the living room as he awoke and craned his neck. A soft glow of lamplight shined over Vale and Cherry, their heads bent where they shared a book on their laps. He squinted. Was that a Bible? The women's voices soft and low, he caught the name of Jesus. The side of his mouth twitched. *Hallelujah!*

He should think of God more often, read the Bible daily, and pray a whole lot. He needed to do this if God decided he would be healed or not.

CALEB LAY ON the living room sofa in a prone position, the weight of a blanket comforted him. How did he get on his back? He sniffed. Food. Greasy food. Yum. He straightened, and he lowered his feet to the cold floor. No migraine. He bowed his head and prayed for God's protection on another day. Where was God's protection when he fell down the mountain? Nope. He wouldn't go there. He prayed for patience.

He sniffed again. Bacon. He imagined the meat in Nana's large cast iron fry skillet. And a pang of sorrow slammed into his chest. The fall on Mt. Baldy knocked the wind from him then, much like his emotions did now. He had been closer to Nana than to Papa.

When would his heart stop its ache?

His eyes roamed the wall hangings, knickknacks, and family portraits. All Nana's touches. Everything the same since his earliest memories. He shook his head and inhaled. Nana was gone. Papa was gone. And he had to accept this and concentrate on healing, although he would always miss them.

He headed to his bedroom, and shifted gears about the biggest challenge in his life. Did he really have the faith in Christ to withstand much more of the migraines? And time would tell if the essential oils did their job. Was it wrong to hope something so simple could help? He snatched from his duffle bag a clean camouflage T-shirt and green cargo pants.

About his wobbly faith. He'd try for Apostle Paul's faith, but that saint was a faith-walking machine.

What does it take to achieve this?

Only time would tell on that one.

However, he wanted to go back in time, and for the pain to melt like snow on warm day. More than anything, he longed to rewind to the day on the mountain. If only his moccasin had not slipped on the loose rocks. If only he had tested the rocks to assure they would not shift beneath his weight. Dumb. Really dumb.

He showered, dressed, and snuck into the kitchen. By the empty shells on the counter, Vale had apparently whipped her ma's goose eggs in a bowl. He grabbed her waist. "Gotcha!"

The fork flew. Hit him on the nose. Gooey, orange egg drip-dropped along his chin.

Her face molted into a shade of pink bubblegum. "Caleb Josiah Cutter." She crossed hands over her heart. "You about killed me with fright."

Laughter rumbled in his chest. He slapped his hands on bent knees and laughed harder.

Cherry skidded into the kitchen on stocking feet. "What? What are you guys doing?"

He gazed at her curly, ginger hair tweaked around her face. Her eyes puffy from sleep. She couldn't have looked prettier. Was that an overlong T-shirt she wore with a red-haired mermaid painted on the front? He swiped off the egg with his fingers. "Ah, Vale's jumpy."

"Am not." She stared at Cherry. "How would you like it if you were deep in thought beating eggs and someone grabbed you from behind?" She put her arms in front of her and curved her fingers into claws. "Grrr."

"I wouldn't." Cherry pointed at him and giggled. "You've been slimed."

He took a washcloth and wiped off the rest of the egg. He rushed at Cherry and waggled the dirty cloth at her face. She reared back and yawned. "You guys woke me. Is it really time to get up?"

Vale waved a wooden spoon over the set table and pursed her lips at Cherry.

"Okay then." Cherry blinked. "Be right back."

She pointed to the refrigerator. "Get the juice, Caleb."

He bowed. "Yes, oh—" His head spun, he stumbled, and grabbed the counter. His whole body weaved. "Whoa."

"Dizzy spell?" She clutched his elbow and her brows scrunched. "Maybe if you wash your face with warm water, you'll feel better."

He moved to the kitchen sink. Grateful the migraine had not come back, yet. But. How could he go hunting when he was a dizzy man?

13~YOU ARE WITH ME
VALE

NANA'S AND PAPA'S bedroom. Vale retreated there after breakfast while the sun broke the dawn. Poor Caleb's face had grown as pale as a full moon. She maneuvered to the end of the bed and tucked in the sheet. She caressed the top quilt, and visions surfaced as to when Nana made this one. All stitched on a non-electric peddle sewing machine.

Ancient. Like Nana.

She shut the door and her knees hit the floor at the bedside and she folded her hands. Her whispers were for an audience of One. "Dear Father, please, Lord, let the oils help Caleb. He needs a break. Heal him from his head pain." She paused. *I'm afraid about his taking this medication.* "Help him to trust You."

A knock rapped on the bedroom door.

"Through Jesus' name, I ask. Amen." She got off the floor and opened the door and it creaked on its hinges. Cherry's soft smile showed off a bit of pink braces. "Thank you, Vale, for clearing away some of my confusion I had about what church attendance means." She shrugged.

Vale sat on the bed and patted it next to her. Once Cherry settled, Vale folded her hands on her camouflaged-jeaned lap. "Do you believe God can heal Caleb?"

"Well, sure." Her eyes searched Vale's as though she wondered about the question.

She sighed and rested an elbow on her knee, cheek cradled in her palm. "If I understand scripture, God can choose to heal or not as we pray in faith for His will."

"Okay." Cherry scratched the crown of her head with a slender finger.

Vale knew faith by heart from Nana's teachings. From the Bible stories Ma read to her every night. But to put it to practice? Vale straightened her back and squared her shoulders. "So, let's pray individually for Caleb." She slid Cherry a glance. "Agreed?"

Cherry cupped Vale's hands with her own and her face beamed.

"Good." She slipped her hands free. "Now let's get the horses ready. You and Caleb are taking a ride."

She gasped, and her mouth formed an O. "I thought you two were going on a hunt."

"We will." Vale led the way into the kitchen. "Tomorrow."

"But what will you do?"

She motioned to the four walls. "I'll find plenty to clean in this cabin alone, and that's not even counting the grounds. Nana and Papa usually kept up the property but—" She lowered her lashes. "Now that they're gone it's up to Caleb and me, and he can barely meet the deadlines of his wood orders these days."

"You guys have been going through tough times."

"We have." Vale pulled a loaf of whole-grain bread from the bread box. "Here. Make a picnic lunch. Luncheon meats are in the fridge."

Cherry grinned. "Thanks." Her smile slipped. "I don't know what he likes."

"If you make it, he will eat it."

"Ah, what a guy."

A masculine snort came from behind them. "I'll eat anything." He moved closer. "I'll help, Cherry."

A lump formed in Vale's throat. *Yeah, he's a great guy.*

She grabbed her jacket off Nana's rocking chair and headed for the door. Kippy followed as she yapped at her heels. She flicked her fingers at the dog. "Stop, you hyper mutt." Kippy circled her and tore off toward the barn. Vale blew the air from her lungs. "What does it take to get a little peace?" She opened the barn door and looked back at Kippy across the road. The dog barked in frantic tones beneath an oak tree and sprang into the air like a trick dog for a Frisbee.

Cold snaked along Vale's spine.

That's no Frisbee.

She moved her vision from the trunk of the tree to the largest lower branch. There, a cinnamon cub squirmed into view. As silently as she could, Vale took a backward step and scanned the woods in each direction.

She fast walked toward the cabin and muttered, "Where are you mama bear?" The hairs on the back of her neck prickled.

Once on the porch, she shoved open the door. "Bear cub." She ran to the stone fireplace and lifted one of two rifles from above the mantel. She whirled to face forward and rammed into Cherry.

The whites of Cherry's eyes grew large. "Be careful, Vale."

"Where?" Caleb stepped near their huddle.

Vale jabbed a finger in the direction of the driveway where Kippy let go another string of high-pitched yips. "On a limb in the smaller oak across the road."

"Dang. We've got to call off Kippy before she's bear food. Stay put, Cherry." He grabbed the second rifle from above the fireplace and bolted. "Kippy, girl, come!"

Over Caleb's shoulder, Vale had a good view of the dog. When he moved closer, Kippy's yips became hysterics.

Caleb raised his rifle. Vale did the same. They both covered the areas around the cabin and should soon see mama bear.

A few seconds later the cousins stood back-to-back, the cub's raspy howl split the air over Kippy's cries. *This is it.* She released her rifle's safety and it clicked.

How had the bear and her cub gotten separated?

If the mama bear wasn't anywhere nearby. She blinked. No. Couldn't let down her guard. She had to assume. No ifs. At any moment mama bear's gallops would crash from the tree-lined woods. Vale's heart kicked.

Caleb waved at her and pointed to the back of her. When she hid halfway behind a tree, he nodded and disappeared to the side of the barn. Her stomach somersaulted.

Ahhh, she didn't want to lose sight of him. But she shook off her nauseated imaginings. He, a seasoned hunter, was taught by the best.

A reverberating *crack*.

At a blast, her spine rippled. She twirled in a circle and checked for any sign of the bear. Nope. She flicked on the safety and followed to where Caleb disappeared around the barn.

He laid in a heap on the dirt his rifle next to him.

SHE QUIVERED, SQUATTED next to him, and leaned her rifle against the barn slats. "Caleb." Silence. He faced away from her on his side. *Oh, no. Oh, no.* She pulled him by the shoulder, and he settled on his back. She gasped. A bullet had grazed a trail along the side of his forehead.

He moaned and blood dripped from the wound.

He's alive. She took a clean hanky from her back pocket and pressed it to his head.

Cherry appeared next to them. "Oh, dear Lord, what happened?"

He moved his head and touched the hanky. "Stupid," he croaked.

Vale nibbled on a fingernail, and glanced around. No mama bear in sight.

A snorted growl came from the direction where the cub waited in the branches. A rude word spewed from Caleb's mouth.

Kippy stopped yapping and appeared from the corner of the barn. She halted near Caleb. The dog licked his face, and Vale grabbed hold of her collar.

Cherry knelt, and Vale nudged the dog toward Cherry. "Hold her collar and don't let go."

Her senses on high alert, Vale reached for her rifle as Cherry began to sob. "Shhh," Vale hissed. "Take care of Caleb and Kippy." She viewed their surroundings and ignored Cherry's mutterings. They were at a disadvantage. If the bear caught a whiff of their scent? She'd gallop to where they hid . . . there'd be only a few yards between them and one angry mama. Before Vale could pull the trigger. Before the bear would attack.

Caleb whispered, "Go wide."

She nodded, kept her finger close to the safety. She crouched and headed to the tree line. She could stay in view of Caleb and Cherry, and yet watch the cub. She'd see mama bear soon enough. Once there, she hid behind an old-growth fir tree and waited for the bear to make her next move.

Ever so sneaky, Vale peered in slow motion at every direction of the woods. Soon, her eyes focused on a large, furry backside. Vale stilled, inhaled a deep breath, and eased it on the exhale.

Mama bear whirled.

Black-beady eyes stared. Right. At. Vale. *She smells me.*

When the mama lifted her front paws and stood, Vale's chin followed her height. Seven foot, eight foot tall? The bear roared and the sides of her lips flapped. Vale's scalp prickled as though stuck by a thousand needles. She steadied her weapon against her right shoulder and pinned the crosshairs on the mama bear's heart. Her finger clicked off the safety, and she kept her index finger at the side of the trigger. *Shallow breaths. Please Lord. Help.*

If this bear took one step toward Caleb, even though the cub needed her, Vale would fire. Because she'd heard the stories. The ones from her Native American ancestors from generation to generation. The stories Papa shared. How bears can outrun a human. How hard he said it was to stop a bear even after more than one shot. He also told Caleb and her when they took up archery, always carry your pistol when you bow hunt. It takes a mighty accurate hit to bring down a bear with an arrow. You need a pistol for backup or better yet a rifle.

Mama bear's teeth clicked.

Vale broke into a sweat and willed her hands to hold the rifle steady. *I can do all things through Christ.* Mama bear did not move.

The cub, though, lowered its head. He wagged it from side to side and seemed to understand he was no longer in danger of Kippy. The little guy scrambled backward down the tree. When the cub jumped to the ground, the mama twisted away from Vale's direction. She nosed her baby and swung her paw. *Slap!* The youngster fell hard on his furry behind. The leaves around him puffed and scattered. The cub shook his head from the smack. Mama bear angled her position, lumbered into the trees, and the cub followed in a gallop.

Vale stared at the spot where mama bear had stood. She let go a shaky sigh and, on legs as limp as a spring fawn, walked toward her cousin.

Slumped on the ground, Cherry leaned against the barn. "Is it gone?"

Vale rested her rifle against the wood slats. "Yeah, she and the baby both."

Caleb used his rifle to help himself to stand. "You did well, Vale. And I'm glad you didn't panic and shoot the mama. The cub looked a bit young to live without her."

"I would have taken a shot if she charged." Vale wiped the sweat on her upper lip across her sleeve. "Man." She released her breath in a *swoosh* of air. "I've never been so scared."

Cherry's mouth quivered. "Well, if it had been me, I would have shot her anyway."

Vale studied her, not sure she heard her correctly. "What?"

"You were taking such a chance, and Caleb unable to walk." She glared back as though to hit home her point.

Caleb reached for her hand to help her stand. "Cherry."

She faced him and squinted. "That was too risky, and it didn't have to be so, so, *drawn out.*"

Vale did not bite her tongue. "Your point being?"

"I just think." She crossed her arms. "So okay. I admit it."

The cousins shared a glance. "What?"

Her bottom lip extended in a pout. "I'm too embarrassed."

"Come on, Cherry." She blinked and shook her head. "So what if you were scared. I just told you I've never been so scared, didn't I?"

Caleb used his arm to swipe at the blood on his face. "Yeah, me too."

Tears rolled along Cherry's cheeks. "I'm still sitting here, uh, I've . . ."

Vale waved a hand in the air. "Spit it out, Cherry."

"But," she whispered, "I wet my pants."

Vale blinked.

"Let's go inside." Caleb slipped his hand into Cherry's. "There's no shame in being afraid, especially when it comes to a mother bear and her cub."

She sniffled.

Vale stared at them, while Cherry shuffled toward the house. Sure enough, she had a stain on her backside the size of a soccer ball. *Poor thing.*

Vale gathered the two rifles, so grateful for how the bear incident ended. Inside the barn, she scooped grain into the horse feeder. "Welp, Princess, what a day." She dumped grain into the other feeder for Storming and groomed Princess. Vale sucked air through her teeth. "I can't count how many times as a kid that I wet my pants from giggle fits."

She finished brushing Princess and moved to Storming when Caleb came into the barn. He had a bandage on the side of his forehead. She aimed her chin at his wound, still unnerved by his mishap. "What happened exactly?"

He covered the bandage with his hand. "You think Cherry's situation is embarrassing. Mine's worse." He stared at her.

She stilled the horse brush on Storming's back. "Do tell."

"Not a soul. Okay?"

"I won't."

"I . . . tripped. On a rock. The gun fired when it hit the ground."

"Your safety was *off*?"

"Yeah." He scratched his ear. "Real dumb."

"Ya know." Vale shuddered. "You've become accident prone." Tears stung behind the bridge of her nose. "And this scares me, Caleb."

"Tell me about it."

She glanced at the cabin and needed to change the subject before she burst into tears. "How's she doing?"

"I think it pretty much did her in." He scratched his earlobe. "She's just not used to the wilds."

She continued to brush Storming. "I know, but she's really trying."

Caleb rubbed a hand over his horse's black coat. "She thinks she needs to go home."

"Whatever." She dug out a burr from Storming's mane. "I don't blame her." This was her and Caleb's yearly hunting trip. Not Cherry's. Now, to admit this made her ashamed. Again. Jealousy. Never right. She handed the brush to him. "Will you finish brushing Storming? I'll go talk to her."

As Vale walked away, he said, "Thanks, Cuz."

"You're welcome," she whispered into the autumn air.

She'd help Caleb and Cherry for only one reason. Those two were falling in love faster than a boulder could roll down a cliff. Was she really such a sap when it came to love? A vision of Dr. Peterson popped into her mind. Vale rolled her eyes to the heavens. *Deliver me, Lord.*

VALE LEANED INTO the door jamb of the bedroom she and Cherry shared. Cherry stuffed a pair of sandals into a duffle. Her wet hair dripped as she bent over the bag. Yep, she would have needed a shower after the uh, unmentionable accident.

She placed her hands on her hips and cleared her throat with an *uh, huh*.

"Oh." Cherry jerked. "You scared me." She fingered her makeup bag. "I'm too—" Her cheeks flushed crimson.

Vale flapped a hand as though to swat a fly. "Happens to the best of us."

She raised her brows. "Really?"

"I know so. I wet my pants lots of times."

Cherry shook her head once both ways. "But you were a child, right?"

"The last time?" Vale wrinkled her nose. "Seventeen."

Cherry twisted her mouth to one side and blinked.

"Yes." She held up a finger. "And Caleb knew how to make me giggle so hard, I sometimes didn't make it to the bathroom in time."

"Oh."

Vale rested her moccasin on the footboard of the bed. "So, you understand."

"I do."

She raised her brows. "Sooo, you're leaving early?" She waved a hand at Cherry's bag.

"My nerves are toast." She lowered her lashes. "But the truth is I do want to horse-back ride."

"Get ready then, lady." She lowered her foot to the floor and slapped her thigh. "Don't keep a good guy waiting."

Her eyes gleamed and she spun in a circle. "Am I dressed for it?" She pointed at what Vale figured were her newer jeans.

"Why not? Though—" She dug through Cherry's suitcase. "You need to dress in layers this time of year." She held a deep-red plaid flannel. "What about this?"

Cherry added the button-down shirt over her tee. She waved at Vale. "Thanks." She hurried out the door. But before Vale could leave the room, Cherry rushed back in and gave her a quick hug, twirled, and left again.

A chuckle rose to her throat. Cherry had grown on her like a flavorful cup of hot Irish tea sweetened with goat milk.

But.

She frowned. Would Cherry flirt and afterward break a heart?

THE TWO LOVE doves rode off on the horses, and Vale lost her desire to clean. Instead, she wanted to pray for her cousin. She knelt by the bed again. "Lord, please, please help Caleb, and allow the essential oils to ease his pain. In Jesus' name. Amen."

She crawled onto the bed, stretched, and read a historical novel about a young white woman living among a Native American tribe. Her eyes grew bleary and her lashes drooped. She dreamed Storming stumbled beneath Caleb's weight on a steep, steep trail. It sent him and the horse headlong down a cliff. Vale screamed and woke.

Tears clung to her eyelids. A nauseated lump formed in her stomach, and she forced herself to rise from the bed. Chamomile tea would calm her nerves.

Near dark, Caleb and Cherry still hadn't returned. Vale grew more uneasy by the second. Why would they still be out unless— Like in her dream? Vale headed for the gun rack and grabbed her rifle once again. She loaded it and hurried outside. Right as she opened the Jeep's door someone's laugh rang in the air.

Cherry.

Vale released a long breath and checked the gun's safety. Yep. Still on. She rested the butt of the gun on the front edge of her moccasin. She wanted to complain at how worried she had been. Instead, she whirled around and headed to the cabin as though her nerves weren't as stiff as taut leather.

The love birds came inside a half hour later.

Her hands stilled over the preparation of supper, and her gaze traveled the length of the both of them. *Soaked to their thighs.* "What happened to you?"

Cherry giggled. "I fell off your horse and took a dunk into the creek."

"Got any bruises?"

"She should." Caleb grinned. "I had to rescue her."

"You sure did." Cherry took a step toward the entryway from the kitchen. "I need to change and finish packing. Gotta work Monday." But she walked closer to Vale, while Caleb snatched a piece of garlic bread off the counter.

Vale moved to where the food warmed on the stove. "If you don't have time to eat before you leave, I can pack your supper, and you can eat it when you get home."

Cherry leaned closer to the stove. "That would be wonderful."

She rummaged through a cupboard and chose a plastic bowl and its lid and filled it with food. "I hope you don't mind leftover spaghetti and meatballs and sourdough garlic bread."

She clapped. "My favorite. I'll eat the bread on the way home." Cherry reached for her arm. "Thanks, Vale. You made me feel welcomed." Her eyes shimmered.

Were those tears? Warmth crept along her neck at Cherry's emotions. She really did seem to like Vale. "I'm glad you enjoyed it, except for maybe the bear."

"It'll make me tougher, now won't it?" Cherry waved her off as she moved from the kitchen. "I'll get my bags."

After she left, Vale leaned close and whispered in Caleb's ear, "I think overall she's right for you."

"Thanks." He play-socked her arm and grinned. "I'll help carry her luggage."

A groan rumbled in her chest when he disappeared through the kitchen entry. Did she really mean it about Cherry being right for him? Or had she become too hopeful for his happiness? At Cherry's show of emotion? She could only hope and pray this worked for him, because it was obvious Caleb liked her.

A whole lot.

14~ROD AND YOUR STAFF
CALEB

IN THE GRAY of dawn Caleb jerked awake, and his hands shook as he pulled Nana's quilt higher to below his nose. He couldn't wait until he weaned off this medication.

He should have had his papa to help pray for him about the right medication to keep away the migraines. Cherry was correct. This medication was not for him.

He had made a hasty decision.

Caleb sighed. His breath made the edge of the quilt tremble. If only Mom and Dad had lived to help him through this bad patch. Uncle Jack and Aunt Rodell had done a good job when they took him in and finished raising him. But still. He missed his mom. He missed his dad.

An ache in his chest gnawed. He knew friends who had run far and away to break from their elders' control. Caleb's sigh deepened. He didn't understand those friends. They were lucky they had parents. And needed his own, especially now. As he turned on his side, his head pounded—like the cadence of his splitting maul slamming onto the wedge as he swung to split the top of a round log.

Weary to the core, Caleb reached for the lavender oil on the nightstand, dabbed a bit on his finger and massaged it into his temples. Soon, the head pain eased.

Seconds later, Vale called his name. "C'mon, lazy crow. It's time for a serious hunt." She flipped on the bedroom light.

He shielded his eyes with an arm. "I'm up. I'm up."

"Okay, then, birthday guy. I'll make your favorite. Pecan pancakes, bacon, and eggs."

"That's right." He propped up on his elbow. "Happy birthday to you too, Valie."

She stuck her thumb in the air. "Watch out world." She switched off the light and left the room.

Yeah. The world better beware of her, maybe even the universe. In less pain, his chuckle came easily as he swung his legs off the bed. A click, click, click sound grew closer. Kippy's toenails alerted Caleb to her approach as she hurried toward him. She stopped at his feet and wagged her stumpy tail. He finger-combed the long hairs on her back. Despite the promise of a perfect day, his mind stayed in the shadows. He wanted to crawl back under the covers, curl into a ball, and hide.

Instead, he closed his door, and knelt before the bed, and prayed. He would keep his word to talk to God more often. Kippy sniff-sniffed him, and her presence comforted him. He laid all his pain at Jesus' feet, who was the great comforter. He recalled scripture which taught that he was to think on the blessings of his life. No matter the sorrow. Though thinking on the blessings never intended to minimize the hard stuff people went through. It served to keep one's eyes on the Christ.

At least he hoped it worked.

Cherry came to mind. Their friendship was a surprise, and he wanted more for them. Although, Papa said once, "Caleb, be friends first with a lady who might one day be your wife. I did this, and your nana is still my best friend."

He rose to his feet, his spirit a tad lighter. *Is this hope?* He slipped on his moccasins and wiggled his toes. The softened leather was pliable—kind of like him after he prayed.

However, this hope lasted only minutes as he walked into the kitchen to where Vale stood at the stove and broke an egg into the skillet. He shivered. "Why is it so stinkin' cold?"

She shrugged. "I've started a good fire in here." Looking over her shoulder, she tossed an eggshell into the trash. "Do you feel twenty years old?"

"Hmmm, I suppose." He grabbed the glass of orange juice near his plate. "This will chase away the deep-into-my-bones cold." He tossed the juice down his throat in three gulps. To practice seeing the blessings would be hard, especially when he had grown so worn out. Never had his emotions swayed like treetops in a stormy wind.

AT THE FOUR-WAY intersection of the dirt roads, he dug his heels into Storming's sides and clicked his tongue. Vale kept pace next to him as they took a left on the smaller logger road. Seconds into their trot, a rabbit darted a few yards in front of them and ran to the other side of the road.

Soon they came to a body of water and stopped.

They both dismounted and walked over to the other side of the road. "There's our lake."

"Yep." She moved to his side. "We've swam there more times than I can count."

Laid out before them, the small lake shimmered. Green water plants dotted the surface of the water, and he scanned the entire width. They had many great memories here with their grandparents, which included picnics in their canoe and fishing. "Let's go." He led the way to the place where they always tied the horses. They added a lead rope to each horse for them to eat grass in a wide circle, but not too close for them to tangle. Around the lake and into the woods their tree stand waited.

Before they headed to the stand, they sprayed their clothes with a de-scenting spray. This way the bucks had one less reason to spook because of Caleb and Vale's need to be close to them. A bow would not shoot a long distance like a rifle.

Vale capped the spray can and loaded her pack on her back. Caleb double checked that his wire rope was in the bottom of his backpack. He attended to his outer wear and made sure his knife was snug in the sheath on his hip.

At the same time, they grabbed their bows which carried four arrows tucked in their secured slots attached to the side. They removed one of their broad-head arrows and slipped the nock into the string. His fingers tightened on the bow's grip and a powerful sensation tingled over his limbs. They were doing this, and hopefully this time he wouldn't blackout.

They adjusted the pistols at their waists and unsnapped and snapped the holster straps. If either one took a tumble, they needed to know their pistols wouldn't fall from their holsters.

Finished with preparations, the cousins slapped palms together. Her smile grew. "We're buck hunting."

"For the smart and crafty black tail." He yahooed under his breath. "Watch out, boys, here we come."

They stepped onto the logger road which led to the path toward their tree stand. Now if only his migraines would stay gone, at least until the hunt trip was over. Better yet, he needed them to disappear forever.

AS VALE FOLLOWED behind him in soft footfalls, she tapped his shoulder. "Stop," she whisper-hissed.

He halted, scanned the area, and glanced back. His lips formed a silent, "What?"

She whispered, "I don't hear it now."

"What did it sound like?"

"Shuffling." Her fingers flicked as though to shoo him onward.

He was glad to keep on the move because his head did not hurt. Nor was he dizzy. Maybe the medication took longer to work than anyone thought. Maybe his headaches were gone for good. Maybe, just maybe, God had chosen to heal him. *Or is it possible the essential oils did the trick?*

As they kept a steady pace, their moccasins remained silent. All the while a breeze stirred and blew in their favor. In their faces. Away from the bucks, and that they hopefully headed toward. As they headed closer to their path and the trees stand, the deer would not smell them. Even if any odor remained after they sprayed with descent spray. The only way they would be busted by a buck in this wind direction was if they did not move along like quiet slugs.

A sudden movement rustled the leaves on the embankment near them. Vale raised her bow in slow motion. Caleb copied the maneuver just in case it was at least a forked-horn buck.

Again the leaves rustled nearby. As was their customary way, he allowed Vale to get first try at their game. Ladies first wasn't just a cliché. She moved along the path in baby steps and then halted.

The animal snorted and grunted. Now twigs and limbs snapped. Caleb sniffed the air. No stench of a bear. Still, with slow movements he unsnapped his pistol holster.

Vale nodded her head for him to come closer to the embankment and to her right. They were a few yards apart when he stopped alongside. "Buck" she mouthed. Leaves, twigs, and limbs shuffled, and she edged closer to the sound.

They both knew the area well. Where they focused on a short distance, there was a bench of ground and passed that a flat area. No big trees, only a few sapling firs, and a perfect place for a buck to serenade a doe.

Beyond this bench area was where the logger road wound around and continued. On the other side of the road, a sheer cliff drop. If they scared the buck in that direction, they would lose him into the dense wilderness.

As sudden as it had begun, the buck's dance stilled. So did the cousins. Frozen like statues. Vale now edged closer. Her bow aimed. He knew why she hadn't pulled back the string. She wouldn't until her target was a kill shot. No one wanted to wound an animal only to have it wander off and possibly suffer an agonizing death.

The loud *whoosh* from the buck's nostrils shot electric zings throughout Caleb's body. The buck's dance ratcheted in fervor. All the while, the cousins drew closer. The wind still blew light and met their faces.

Perfect.

They were at the outer edges of where the sun's rays shone on the clearing. They both stopped. He moved sideways to close the gap between them. The buck's hooves continued to rustle.

When the rustle and stomp moved away and continued, the cousins pinned each other in a glance. He pointed for her to enter.

The moment she stepped into the edges of the clearing, the two deer quieted. He followed and halted beside her. They didn't dare enter. It would only spook the deer into a run.

The cousins' arms touched, he breathed in shallow breaths. She crouched. Caleb did the same. He gazed at the clearing and beyond until his eyes focused on darker shadows which became shapes in the brush. A neck and shoulders. The head and antlers were hidden, but the buck's swollen neck could not be denied. Caleb appreciated how God had created bucks so their hormone glands caused their necks to swell and signaled mating season.

Were the antlers at least forked or branched? And then the buck turned his head. These antlers were many more than a fork. Caleb's heart ratcheted.

Vale nodded, aimed, and pulled the string, elbow extended. If the buck stayed, it would be a good shot to the— But before he completed the thought, the buck jerked to the right. His hooves rustled across the ground. When he moved, he exposed a shadowy form. The doe. She was a beauty. Light gray coat, her eyes shimmered in semi-darkness.

The doe darted into denser shrubbery and stopped inside the thicket. The buck's snorts grew louder. The antlers became visible, and Caleb counted five on one side and six on the other. He pulled the bowstring to assist Vale's shot. If she missed.

The buck had to know they were there, but a buck when he courted a doe became careless. Wreckless enough to cost him his life. And he may have pursued her for quite a while, so wasn't willing to lose his doe. Normally, a buck's need to survive was his main goal. He demanded his nose to smell. Eyes to see. Muscles to sprint.

Not this guy. Not at this moment.

And Caleb's tongue secreted juices at the thought of the meat. Today, this bruiser would be theirs.

Vale's arrow flew in a soft twang. The buck leaped upward and disappeared and his doe followed. Vale whooped a holler. "I got him in his lower shoulder."

As Caleb wiped the sweat from his brows, his mouth quirked. "Big fella. Hope the meat isn't tough."

"I counted his antlers, a five-by-six, right?"

"Exactly."

The cousins released deep sighs and chuckled. Vale waggled her palm in the air. He slapped his palm against hers. They grabbed their flashlights from their backpacks and began to track the buck from the spot where she shot him. There on the leaf-covered ground lay a spatter of blood. Because it was darker under the shadow of tree limbs, they switched on their flashlights. There to the left, the trail of blood grew thick. He pointed at her watch.

"Umm, almost eleven. We should have plenty of daylight to field dress the buck and bring the carcass to the horses."

"Sweet. Let's go."

Vale slapped him on the back. "This is the biggest buck I've ever taken down."

The cousins headed toward a dead end at the steep side of the cliff.

THEY PEERED DOWN the embankment. A logger road thirty yards below. "Shall we?" Caleb readjusted his billed hunting hat. He sat on his behind and pushed his moccasin feet in what he thought as an easy slide. In a blink, he slipped. He tumbled the rest of the way, shoulder to back in a roll. Caleb hit the road feet first and stumbled to upright. His breath gushed. *Swoosh.* "That smarted."

Vale slid down to the road, rose, and walked toward him. "Since when do you try out for the circus?"

He touched his neck and began to massage. "I could have broken something." He sat on the hard ground.

A canteen came into view, and she pressed it to his mouth. He gulped and swallowed.

"We should get you back to the cabin." Her brows furrowed. "I'll get the horses and bring them the long way on the road."

Caleb snatched her shirt sleeve. "Wait." The line between her brows deepened. "Give me a minute, will you?" He swiped the dirt-encrusted sweat off his forehead. "I'm not hurt."

"No, Caleb." She swiveled. "The buck can wait."

This time he grabbed her arm.

She shook off his hold and placed her hands on her hips. "You mule-headed stubborn—" She waved a hand at his feet. "You're so wobbly, you can barely stand."

"I just rolled down the embankment. Of course I'm wobbly." He lowered his chin to rest for a moment. "Zip it."

Her whine came soft as though she had bumped her shin or stubbed her toe. She settled next to him on the red dirt. "You keep getting hurt."

"I know. It's your job to mother me. Or smother me. Give it a break, though." He pressed his lids closed. "Please, Vale."

Her arm brushed his.

He cocked open one eye.

She held a stick and used it to scribble on the ground. They sat in silence for long minutes. Vale sniffed. He pulled his knees closer to his chest and wrapped his arms around them. At least his head didn't pound. He'd take a body ache fall any day over another bonk to the head.

Soft words floated from her, "Please, Lord, help." She touched his moccasin closest to her and patted.

His lips parted. Her simple prayer cut straight to his heart.

15~COMFORT ME
VALE

"READY?" CALEB GRIPPED her hand and held on while she tugged. She whispered, "You scared the breath right out of me, Cuz."

"I know." He brushed the dirt off his camouflage jeans.

She readjusted her hand on her bow. "What do you wanna do?" *Please say go back.*

"Retrieve our buck."

"Oh." Her voice sounded as hollow as an rotted-out log. She had to stop the mother role which he claimed smothered him and never helped. She'd try a buddy tone. "How's the pain?"

"Better."

She wanted to believe he felt well enough to follow the trail of blood, so she pasted on the fakest grin this side of the Rogue River. "Let's track."

He took the lead and said over his shoulder, "Would you double check the ground behind me? Make sure I'm going the right way." He reached the other side of the logger road first where it dropped off. He sidestepped his way down and she followed, though this precaution never guaranteed a person wouldn't stumble and dive into the dirt. Or go off a cliff. Her knees shook.

She drew in a deep breath at his double-checking comment. *Are his eyes blurry?* As she began her descent, the side of her moccasin snagged on what felt like a root. Her hands flew in front of her, and she tumbled. As she fell, she met Caleb, and he grabbed at her arm. A useless attempt as her shirt stretched and ripped. Her fall lasted forever until she banged into an unforgiveable object. *Swoosh.* It knocked the breath clear from her lungs. She wheezed. Vale flickered her eyelids but slammed them shut against the dust. Her fingers touched the hard surface. *Boulder.*

She struggled for air, spit, sputtered, and gagged the dirt from inside her mouth. "Vale?" Caleb continued to holler. She wanted to respond, but her lungs gasped for each tiny bit of air. *I'm here. I'm here.*

Vale dug her elbows into the dirt and dragged herself toward the top of the boulder. On each scoot she inhaled and exhaled until she had gained better breaths. But her ribs. Man, did they hurt. Her hand stalled in a tacky puddle. She kept her eyes shut as she brought her palm to her nose and sniffed and swiped the goo on her thigh. Blood. The bucks or hers? Her limbs quivered as she patted her body the best she could for any signs of scrapes or gashes. Nothing.

Now what should she do? She had to see.

All the while Caleb hollered her name.

She pulled her loosened shirttail from her waistband and wiped at her closed lids as the dirt fell. She blinked, blinked, blinked, and opened one eye to a mere slit. The grit caused pain which helped her eye to moisten. The moisture worked to rid the scum from her vision, and the trail of blood came into view as a blur. She worked on the other eye. The red drops came into view now and the trail ended near a red-barked Manzanita bush in its soft-green and silver-leaves.

Was her vision playing tricks? A fur rump and tail protruded from underneath the Manzanita. The branches and leaves covered the rest of the buck to his head and antlers.

I found him.

She studied her surroundings. The boulder she slammed into perched on the side of the cliff. Below her, the Rogue River tumbled and rushed. She gulped. A wave of dizziness followed. The boulder saved her life. Her body shook at the very idea that she almost fell to her death. She had to crawl to the top of the boulder before she'd be safer.

"Vale! I see you. Don't move. I'll come to you."

Dirt clods and small rocks slapped at her and hurled alongside and brought more dust into her nostrils. The pressure of the debris moved the loose dirt beneath her. She slipped. Reached for a knob on the boulder. Missed. Vale slid. On her way down, she grabbed a fistful of thick grass. That halted her fall as her feet and legs flailed in nothing but air. A scream gurgled in her throat. *Oh, God, oh, help!*

16~ANOINT MY HEAD
CALEB

CALEB TOOK SEVERAL steps to reach Vale as pebbles and rocks shifted and slid in her direction. Her scream froze his feet.

Rocks hit her? What should he do now? Caleb's body shivered even though it was a warm day. *Get control, get control. For Vale's sake.*

He shouted, "I'll throw down the wire rope." He heaved himself back up to the top, dug into his backpack, and approached a small tree. The tree ought to easily hold her, and it was close to the embankment to give her enough rope. He hoped.

But Caleb shouted, *"Dang it."*

His fingers fumbled as he wrapped the rope around the tree and a few limbs to secure it. *Hang on, Valie.* Once he had the end of the rope tight on the tree, he blew a deep breath from his lungs and hollered, "How are you holding up, Vale?" He strained to hear as he wrapped the other end of the rope around a rock. The weight on the rope should make it fall to its full length. He hoped it was long enough. He hoped it would not get tangled. He hoped it wouldn't hit her and knock her out.

Her voice was muffled. "Hurry."

"Valie! Guard your head. I've wrapped the rope around a rock. Here it comes."

"I'm off the edge!"

Caleb startled. He recovered though and slung the rope.

Would he be able to rescue Vale?

17~MERCY
VALE

HER GUT CRAMPED. Nausea slid north from her stomach and threatened to invade her throat.

Could this get any worse?

She fluttered her lashes as one set of toes settled on what felt like a tiny ledge on the face of the cliff. Thank the Lord the bunch of wild grass held solid as a cord. But Vale grew tired, shaky, and sweat dripped into her eyes. How much longer could she balance on one leg and hang on to the grass?

God, please.

That's all she had left. If God decided it was her time . . .. Poor Ma. Daddy. Caleb. Dr. Peterson's brown eyes appeared in her mind. Regret surged through her at what may never be.

Her leg which kept her on the ledge quivered. Pain jabbed at that ankle and shot up her calf.

Both hands fisted the grass. The fact the grass held her caused her eyes to moisten in awe of God. Once again, she was grateful for His amazing wonders. But. *Don't throw up.* She gritted her teeth and swallowed the bile.

Caleb's voice called to her. Something about a rope. *Lord.*

As she waited for Caleb to rescue her, a new realization slammed through her thoughts. Now who was saving who?

The back of her nostrils stung from a rush of tears.

Ever since they were ten, when Caleb came to live with them, she had been the protective one. Oh, he was protective when necessary, like most guys. But she nurtured him daily. When he first came to their home after his parents died, she even spoke for him those first few weeks. Anytime Ma asked him a question, Vale had the answer. And Caleb allowed it.

"Valie!"

She didn't dare. Don't. Look. Up.

"Guard your head. I've wrapped the rope around a rock. Here it comes."

In seconds, dirt trickled past, and pebbles hit her upper body. Her head still bowed, a clod bumped her crown and bounced off her shoulder. All the while, she squeezed her eyes shut. When debris no longer fell, Vale peeked up.

She raised her chin above the wild grass bunched in her hands and scanned the area. There. Right there. The rock still tied to the rope was within a foot of her left hand. But her belly squeezed at the idea of even one hand not attached to the tough grass. She whimpered. *I can't.* More sweat pooled under her arms.

You can do all things through me.

Lord? She pursed her mouth and swallowed.

She rose on her toes upon the ledge, stretched herself toward the rock, and her left hand reached, reached . . .. A mere few inches from her grasp. *I can do all things through Christ which strengthens me.*

Dig the dirt.

She nodded and rested first. Then she stretched, clawed at the dirt below the rock, the rock rolled and bopped her on the chin. She'd have a bruise but Vale grinned. She thanked the Lord with her whole being.

ONCE VALE HAD the rock in both hands, and lifted herself off the ledge, she hollered, "Pull me up."

As her hips passed the big boulder, she yelled, "Stop." She placed her feet on the boulder and breathed deeply. "We did it, Lord. Thank You." Her nausea eased, and her heart warmed at how much God loved her. Had He really spoken to her spirit? She shook her head and decided to think on that later tonight when she lay safe in bed.

"Are you okay?"

"Yes, Caleb. Let me gain my strength."

"Okay. Give me a holler when you're ready for me to pull again."

While Vale rested, she studied the buck's hind end. She held the rope by the rock and squirmed on her stomach and thighs as her knees moved her closer to the carcass. *Slap.* Her right hand fastened on a root closer to the buck.

Could she do it? Could she bring herself up to Caleb and take the buck also? She raised her voice. "Caleb. I'll see if I can loop the rope around the buck's hooves."

"Forget. The. Buck."

Did he growl at her? "I'm bringing him." *Sheesh. Icing on the cake after I almost died.*

"Dad-gummit, Vale. You better be right about this. So help me."

The rock became taut in her hand and she hung on. "Okay, I'm moving." In slow motion, she walked on her knees nearer to the buck's hind end. Her sore ankle hit a rock. She winced and sucked air through her teeth. She kept going. When she made it next to the carcass, she hollered, "I'm at the buck." Vale peered around and through the narrow space of the Manzanita.

"How are you doing?"

"Good. I'll attach the rope to the buck's hind hooves. I'll crawl under the Manzanita where he's at and get to his head." She paused at an idea. "Wait. I think you should get Storming and have him pull the buck up and then me. That way you won't be overusing your muscles and wear yourself out."

"You stubborn girl. You're going to get killed."

He had no idea the worst was behind her. "Trust me." She thought again. "Would you bring Princess also? Just in case I'm too tired to walk." Her ankle pain had increased as well as her ribs.

"Are you safe, then?"

"Yep." Vale brushed at the dirt on her jeans. "Hurry."

She rested again and inspected her sore ankle. *Swelling fast.* She brought her attention to the buck's hoof and inserted it through the loop she had made above the rock. She wrapped the rope around it once and took the other hoof and wrapped it tight against the first hoof. The rock would for sure hold the hooves snug. She examined the deer trail where the buck collapsed. *So narrow.* She'd crawl over the buck if needed. Although—Vale squirmed. Stuck out her tongue. The idea of squishy pressure on a furry stomach sounded gross. Vale studied the space on either side of the buck. She'd break a few smaller branches, crawl over his legs. This way she could push the antlers as Caleb pulled the buck's back hooves upward.

The late afternoon sun beat on her head and shoulders. Flies buzzed. She licked her lips. *Thirsty.*

"Vale? I'm back."

"Good."

"I've got Storming and Princess. Do you think Storming can pulled the buck straight up or is there something blocking the path?"

"A Manzanita." She wiped the sweat from her forehead. "I'm going to have to push the buck's antlers while Storming pulls. Give me about five minutes. I'll whistle when ready."

"Okay."

She crawled two steps and broke a few branches which were right in her face. She moved over the buck's front hooves and broke more limbs. Near the head of the buck there was only about two feet of level ground. She'd have to take great care to not move much past the buck's antlers or she'd slip down the mountain. Again.

She bowed her head. "Please, Lord. Help." Her left ankle had swelled too tight against the leather of her moccasin and throbbed to the beat of her heart. *Here I go.* She moved inch by inch past the buck's head and gripped the antlers. She used her right foot, because every time she put weight on her left she gasped in pain. When Vale was inches past the head, she kept a strong hold on the antlers and twisted her body to face it. An antler pressed her stomach. *Careful.* The antler eased away from her belly. *Watch the ankle. Ow.*

Finally, Vale stuck her middle finger and thumb on each side of the tip of her curled tongue and whistled. But her dry tongue only made a blowing sound. She hollered, "I'm ready, Caleb. Storming should only take one step and stop. It'll be tricky to get this buck from under the brush." She braced her knees on the ground, both hands on the antlers. A spasm of pain radiated from her left ankle, and she closed her eyes. *Oh, oh, oh.*

The rope tugged on Storming's power. Vale pushed. That scooted the buck twelve inches.

"How are you, Valie?"

She wiped her sweaty face on the tail of her shirt. "I'm ready for another pull."

At the rope's jerking motion, Vale's knees buckled and she landed on her stomach. She rose to her knees and judged how far the buck protruded from the brush. They had a long way yet. Her limbs trembled from exhaustion.

"YOU READY, VALE?"

She nodded and braced herself to push again. "Go."

The jerk of the rope was more like four of Storming's steps. Vale lost her balance and fell face first on the ground. "Ugh." She lifted her head and spit dirt from her mouth. She was in the middle of the Manzanita's underbrush. Even though she hadn't been ready for the extra steps, it had pushed the buck a full two feet.

"Vale?"

She grimaced and brought a bit of saliva to her lips. *Spit, spit, spit.* "Yeah?"

"I'm sorry about that. Storming's getting antsy."

"Do it again on my go. The buck is halfway through the brush. Give Storming the reins."

"Okay."

Vale pursed her lips into a knot and gripped the antlers. "Go."

The rope jerked. She pushed the deer with all her strength. One of the buck's antlers got caught on a small limb. "Stop!" The rope slacked.

"Are you okay?" Caleb's shaky voice meant he became frightened.

"Yeah, but an antler is caught. Give me a minute." But the branch was too thick for a hand break. Vale shook her head and pulled her knife from its sheath. *Too whooped to think?* What if she had needed the knife before now? "Hang on, Caleb. I have to cut the limb, and it's going to take a while."

"I wish I could help." He sounded as tired as she felt.

"This should be the last thing to block the buck's body. I'm going to whittle on this branch until it's weak enough, and Storming should be able to break it."

"Holler when ready."

Vale's fingers ached from the V cuts she made deeper into the limb. She stopped a few times and tested the branch until she figured it was weak enough. "Give a jerk and stop." *Snap.* She tossed the branch behind her to remove it from the buck's path.

She yelled, "Go," and Caleb and Storming pulled the buck up. Vale swiped a hand over her upper lip. She rested on a foot-wide deer path, and her left foot began to hurt like it was on fire. Tears slipped from her lashes and slid along her cheeks. Beginning to lose her patience, she sucked air through her teeth and waited for Caleb to throw the rope and tow her out.

"Here you go, Vale, and watch your head again." The rock attached to the rope landed below her.

Within easy reach, she drew up the rope and cupped the rock in both hands. She tugged. "Got it!" She muttered, "Come on, Storming, pull me the rest of the way."

Silently she prayed that this was almost over. As she pushed both feet, pain bristled through her left ankle and shot to her hip. A gurgled scream ripped from her throat.

18~DAYS OF MY LIFE
CALEB

DID VALE JUST cry? *Oh, Lord, please help me to help her.*

Storming snickered. Caleb strained his ears but Vale jerked the rope, again, to signal him to keep going. The horse pawed the ground. Storming moved the rope in a steady pace, the weight on the rope proof it pulled Vale. *Yes.* His aunty always said when things appeared bad, never stop hoping. Don't expect. Hope. Now, he told himself this at every tug along the dirt-encrusted mountain to bring Vale closer.

About a yard from the top and within his sight, she caught a foothold with her right moccasin. Her other foot dangled. Caleb extended his hand and she grabbed hold. The rock settled on the ground as she hobbled and dropped near his feet.

He kneeled and slammed into her in a fierce hug.

"Ow." She frowned.

"Mercy." He gasped. "I'm so glad you're topside."

"Water."

Caleb clicked his tongue. "Come, Storming." The horse nodded his head and pawed the dirt. "Come on, boy."

Storming's long legs drew closer to the cousins. His long neck bent, and his muzzle touched Vale's head. He nickered as he moved his lips over her hair. It seemed to Caleb he made sure she was okay. She reached above her and patted his jaw. "We did it, sweet boy."

Storming blew through his nostrils and made strands of her hair float. He nodded as though he agreed.

At his horse's display of affection, Caleb's eyes misted. A sob bubbled in his chest as he loosened the flap on the saddle bag and grabbed the canteen. He settled next to Vale on the ground. "After you've drank, I'll wash the dirt from your face with a bandana."

"I feel gritty."

He unscrewed the cap. "Are you ready to get off the mountain?"

She tipped the canteen and drank a long swallow. After she finished, she sighed. "Mountains don't agree with us this year."

"Ankle hurt?"

"I'll need help."

He placed his hanky in his palm and reached for the canteen. He soaked it and moved it over her face like he was washing a window.

Vale jerked as though he hit her. "Give me that thing." She took it from him. "You're about to scrub my skin off."

He grinned. "I'm so glad to hear your grumpy voice. Up close."

She rolled her eyes, but a grin twitched at the corner of her mouth. She cleaned most of the dirt from her face, and they rested. Caleb took a half an hour to gut the buck and fifteen minutes to hoist and secure the carcass on Storming's rump behind the saddle. He brought Princess to Vale and gave her a boost where she settled onto the saddle. "Thanks, Caleb."

As the two cousins came to a curve on the logger road, Caleb caught sight of two fawns near the tree line. "Look," he whispered, "to our right."

"I see them."

The fawns didn't move, and they had no spots left on their coats. He spoke in a hushed tone. "They're almost no longer babies."

"Next year they will be yearlings."

The cousins glanced at each other. She nodded. Caleb smiled. "We're no longer teenagers."

"True."

As Vale spoke, one of the fawns flagged its tail and moved into the forest. The other fawn nibbled at the oak-tree acorns along the shoulder of the road. Storming gave a sudden jerk on the reins, his head and ears arched. A noise rustled behind the fawn and it bolted.

A cougar pounced near the fawn in one leap.

Storming raised his front legs, whinnying. Caleb lifted his pistol into the air and pulled the trigger. *Bwhoom!* The big cat rushed into the brush, and the fawn darted in the opposite direction.

THE DEER CARCASS hung in the barn to cure and at Caleb's insistence, he drove Vale to the hospital. When he guided the pickup into the emergency parking lot, he gripped the steering wheel. The last time he was here, he lay prone in an ambulance. He breathed in and out. That seemed like yesterday, though it had been many days ago.

He parked the pickup at the entrance, jumped out, and grabbed a wheelchair. Vale's foot had swollen twice its size, so they had to remove her moccasin. He reached for her arms. "I've got ya, Cuz." He settled her into the chair and wheeled her inside.

Before long, they were in the same cubicle he had been in before. Vale readjusted herself on the narrow cot and sucked in her breath. "The doctor is taking forever." Tears moistened her eyes. "Man, my ankle feels broke."

Caleb patted her arm where he sat next to her in a chair. "Pretty soon you'll get some help."

"It couldn't be soon enough."

Right then, a man entered and halted his steps inside the curtained doorway. "Well, well. We meet again."

Caleb smiled and stood. "Dr. Peterson." He reached out, and the doctor accepted Caleb's hand shake.

"So good to see you, although, Miss Cutter may not agree." Dr. Peterson's eyes reflected the same twinkle from when he spoke to Vale all those days ago. "I hear you injured your foot, Miss Cutter."

"Yeah. Hunting."

"Oh? How did it happen?" Dr. Peterson bent over her bare ankle. As she told the story of her fall, the doctor pressed his fingers on her ankle.

"Ow!" Vale shot straight into a sitting position. "Do you have to be rough?"

"I'm sorry, Miss Cutter." His expressive eyes became soft. "I'll order an x-ray."

She pointed. "It feels broke."

"Actually." He raised a brow. "Broken would be better than a severe sprain. Those take much longer to heal."

Caleb glanced at her. "I didn't know that."

Dr. Peterson wrote something on her chart. "Most people don't. Do you hurt anywhere else?"

She pointed to an area of her left ribs. "Yes, but not as bad as my ankle."

The doctor motioned toward her side. "May I?"

Vale nodded.

His fingertips moved in slow motion over where she had pointed. Then he pressed. She jumped, winced, and pursed her lips. He finished his examination and said, "We'll order an x-ray on your ribs also."

He winked at Vale. "I noticed from reading your chart that today is your birthday."

"Yep." She nodded at Caleb. "It's both our birthdays."

"Ah. You are both twenty."

"We are," they said at the same time.

The doctor stuffed his pen in his front pocket. "Do you have any questions for me, Miss Cutter?"

"Yes. Do you always wink at the female patients?"

Dr. Peterson's neck flushed rosy. To Caleb's way of thinking, she had embarrassed him.

"No." The doctor lowered his head for a moment. "And I'm sorry if I was out of line."

She puckered her lips, the corners twitching into what Caleb knew was a suppressed grin. "You didn't offend me, Dr. Peterson." She fluttered her lashes. "Just call me Vale."

WHAT SEEMED LIKE hours later, the x-ray of her ribs and ankle was done, and she and Caleb waited for the results when the good doctor returned to the cubicle.

"Miss Cutter—"

She flicked her fingers in the air. "Vale."

He cleared his throat. "Okay." His eyes danced. "Vale. The bad news is it looks as though you did fracture your ankle bone." As he talked he flipped on the light of a contraption on the wall and light showed the details of Vale's ankle bone.

"Broke for sure." Caleb shuffled his feet. "Does this mean she'll need a cast?"

"Yes, eventually." The doctor moved closer to her. "The good news is your ribs are not damaged. They are probably bruised enough that you'll need to take it easy. We'll wrap and splint your ankle first, until the swelling is minimized." He placed hands on his hips. "And you cannot put any weight on it until we cast it."

"But." She blinked. "I have to work."

Dr. Peterson sat in the chair next to her. "What does your job require?"

She rose to her elbows. "I clean horse stalls and exercise the horses at a stable."

He shook his head. "Not for a while you won't." He stood. "I'm going to get my nurse to bring in the supplies, and I'll wrap and splint your ankle."

When he left, Caleb sat in the chair. "I think he likes you."

She jerked her head and stared at him. "Maybe I like him too." This time, she grinned.

Caleb crossed his arms. "Do you want me to match make?"

"Absolutely not." She snapped. "I wonder if I'll get to see him when I get the cast."

Dr. Peterson entered the room. "Yes, you may come back here if you prefer. I'll give you a date when the cast needs to go on and make sure I'm the one who attends." His lips creased upward in the corners. "How does that sound, Vale?"

Her eyelashes lowered. "Good, Dr. Peterson."

When the nurse came in with the supplies and Dr. Peterson began to wrap her ankle, Caleb winked at her from where he stood near the curtain. This time, her cheeks flushed pink.

Caleb could almost see the future. He'd be feeling better, once he weaned off the medication and continued the essential oils and found a good acupuncturist. He and Cherry, Vale and Dr. Peterson, would double date. And who knew, maybe there'd be a double wedding for them by next year.

Maybe their children would be raised together and be as close as siblings.

Jean Ann Williams began her writing career in 1994 by reading a stack of books on the craft of writing. Since then, she has published over 300 articles and short stories on the topics of Christianity, health, travel, relationships, family life, Sunday school take-home papers, and the loss of a child by suicide. Jean Ann lives on the coast of Oregon with her husband Jim. On their Fowl Play Farm, she raises two ducks and twelve chickens. In her free time, Jean Ann enjoys reading inspirational books, gardening, and playing Scrabble with her grandchildren. Sometimes Nana wins.

Just Claire

One mother damaged. One family tested. One daughter determined to find her place.

ClaireLee's life changes when she must take charge of her siblings because her mother becomes depressed after a difficult childbirth. Frightened by the way Mama sleeps too much and her crying spells during waking hours, ClaireLee just knows she'll catch her illness like a cold or flu that hangs on through winter. ClaireLee finds comfort in the lies she tells herself and others in order to hide the truth about her erratic mother. Deciding she needs to re-invent herself, she sets out to impress a group of popular girls.

With her deception, ClaireLee weaves her way into the Lavender Girls Club, the most sophisticated girls in school. Though her best friend Belinda will not be caught with the likes of such shallow puddles,

ClaireLee ignores Belinda's warnings the Lavenders cannot be trusted. ClaireLee drifts farther from honesty, her friend, and a broken mother's love, until one very public night at the yearly school awards ceremony. The spotlight is on her, and she finds her courage and faces the truth and then ClaireLee saves her mother's life.

Amazon: https://amzn.to/3nKnzwZ
Just Claire Book Trailer:
https://youtu.be/s8x5lJKZFHU
Goodreads *Just Claire*:
https://www.goodreads.com/book/show/2848 2298-just-claire

Road Trip of Delusion

Fifteen-year-old Kari Rose discovers how much trouble she and her two sisters can get into when they stay at their ancient granny's for spring break. Granny gets a wild-haired notion at three in the morning, and she's leaving with or without them. Kari makes the decision to take her sisters and ride with Granny in her old Cadillac on a five-hundred-mile-long trip north to visit family. Miles down the road, this harmless act finds Granny no longer able to drive, and Kari must take the wheel. Soon after, the four travelers are caught in a freeway-closing-down snowstorm which brings everyone and everything to a standstill.

A second blizzard with catastrophic impact is about to descend upon them, and Kari must determine the best way to find shelter and beat the storm. Will Kari trust her gut instincts and rely upon a complete stranger to lead them to safety?

Amazon: https://amzn.to/2Ivyjz6

God's Mercies after Suicide

What if your child shot himself while you were in the next room? What if you held him as his heart beat for the last time? What if Satan whispered in your ear, "Now where is your God?" Find out how Jean Ann Williams reached out with her spirit and mind to the one true Father. Discover how the Lord God answered her, and walked alongside her in the most difficult grief journey of her life.

Amazon: https://goo.gl/wju4dm
God's Mercies after Suicide **Book Trailer:**
https://youtu.be/yvNDlNHEyok
http://Joshua-mom.blogspot.com/

A Pocket Full of Memories

Mother's Day for Dotty Monteiro begins with four cards and ends with an unexpected turn of events. As she and her husband Pete anticipate phone calls from their five children, she quietly prays for visits and a chance to laugh together as a family and hug her children. But where is Lolly, the daughter who felt displaced when the youngest was born? She hasn't been home for three years. Not a call or a card in so long. What Dotty would give to see her daughter again!

Dotty has a long-time faith in Christ and knows God always hears her prayers. But she also knows sometimes they are met with silence. How will her Mother's Day unfold this year? Will it be a repeat of years past? When will she experience the Mother's Day of her heart's desire?

Jean Ann Williams introduced the young Monteiro children in her previous book, *Just Claire*. Now leap into their future as adults with their own families.

Amazon: https://amzn.to/33ZPmBL

Sincerely Claire

After living in California for almost a year, Claire returns to Oregon with high hopes that seventh grade will be better than sixth. Barely off the school bus, though, trouble smacks her in the head. Literally. Her California bullies! Here?

The Lavender Girls' dads were hired to supervise a local tunnel project, and the families came along. Claire knows to watch her back. But she fears for her hometown friend Lizbeth, who has yet to discover how far the Lavender Girls can take their harassment.

Fudging a little on what her parents would approve of, Claire creates her own club to battle the bullies' evil ploys. What will she do when she must make a choice: an eye for an eye – or turn the other cheek?

Amazon: https://tinyurl.com/cwtckxk2

Covered Mercies

"Covered Mercies" is a short companion book to "God's Mercies after Suicide: Blessings Woven through a Mother's Heart". It is written for the weary-worn griever. This book focuses on how the Lord brought Jean Ann Williams through the early grief years after her son, Joshua's, suicide. She writes about how she and her family managed through the "year of firsts" during holidays and significant observance days.

Jean Ann is transparent with her feelings and writes in simplicity as she tells her story of love and loss of her twenty-five year-old son. She was in the house when Joshua died and felt his last heartbeats. She lived in the house for four more years after, enabling God to reshape her into someone who became stronger in Him.

If you are a mother who has lost a child to suicide or knows someone who has, this book is able to comfort and guide through the most difficult time for any parent. Jean Ann tells her story with sensitivity, and she includes Scripture verses, some of which answers questions she had about her son's afterlife.

Amazon: <u>https://www.amazon.com/Covered-Mercies-Jean-Ann-</u>

27 Characters of the Old Testament: Stories and Activities for Children

To receive a free Kindle, sign up for my newsletter at my Website below. Be sure to post a comment to let me know which book you would like. www.jeanannwilliamsauthor.com

Follow me on  @jeanannwilliams

Get new book updates on Amazon: https://amzn.to/3lOlZbk
Facebook Author Page: https://bit.ly/31lI9iD
Instagram: https://www.instagram.com/jeanann_w/
Goodreads Author Page: https://bit.ly/3j03lvk

27 Character Traits
Of The
New Testament:
Stories & Activities for Children
MATTHEW - REVELATION
Jean Ann Williams
Illustrated by Carley Herlihy